CAPRICORN FACES SCORPIO

Signs of Love #7

ANYTA SUNDAY

Capricorn Faces Scorpio

On a quest for long-lasting love, Capricorn? It may be just over the rainbow.

Grappling with a storm in his heart and feeling like a general failure, Carl Birch flees his problems at home and swaps lives with his 'successful' twin brother. Stepping into the shoes of an accomplished professional pianist adored by the locals feels like a breath of fresh air: he's revered, admired, and described as 'talented' for the first time ever.

It feels good, but it's also *complicated*. He can't actually play the piano to save himself, and everyone he meets wants him to play, and teach, and tune, and give motivational speeches at school assembly . . .

If that's not enough, the local heartbreaker has his dark, judgy eyes on him—eyes that seem to *know*. But also to understand. And, vexingly, to suspect Carl has joined the hordes of groupies swooning after him!

To get out of this spiraling mess, Carl will have to face things—both at home, and in his heart.

Buckle up, Capricorn. You're about to undertake a journey of heart, mind, and courageous spirit.

Set in my own suburb of Wellington, but with the addition of a few made-up locations for story-telling purposes.

In this book, Australia is often referred to in its colloquial forms: Aussie and Oz.

This book uses New Zealand grammar and punctuation.

[The sky] was even grayer than usual.
"There's a cyclone coming . . ."

L. Frank Baum

The Wonderful Wizard of Oz

Chapter One

Carl had never thought of himself as a Dead-End Dude, but he'd heard it from an out-of-town customer upset that his selection of magazines 'lacked journalistic integrity', and now he couldn't quite forget it.

Dead-End Dude. He ran his own convenience store, thankyouverymuch. It had regularly replenished refrigerated drinks and a dairy section, there was a bread and cereal aisle, junk food for on the go, all your bathroom and kitchen whatever, and everything a pet owner would ever need, from anti-flea drips to oversize dog kennels.

Dead-End Dude.

He was practically a lifesaver in his curtain-twitching hometown. How many cakes had he saved with his fresh-from-the-farm eggs? And how much more miserable would the keen-eyed, hardworking policemen of Earnest Point be without his cream donuts? *That* really benefited everyone. Especially those like himself, who might leave their bike a little too close to a fire hydrant every so often. Or ride too fast on the footpath. Or forget their helmet. Or draw a picture of a yawning cat on a lamppost—which should totally be excusable if it makes a crying girl with pigtails laugh again.

Dead End . . .

Carl shook his head and flipped the pages of the mag he was browsing through till he reached the horoscopes. See! Capricorn was the least Dead-End-Dude of the entire zodiac. Practical. Determined. Hardworking. Protective.

Jobs most suitable for a Capricorn: Accountant. He absolutely kept his own books. And updated them every month with his trusty four-colour biro and a highlighter.

Lawyer—he might as well be one considering the times he'd weaselled his way out of fines at the local precinct.

School Hall Monitor—oh, he had to keep an eye on the kids all right. They loved trying to get away with potbellies made of lollies, or attempting to buy beer with straggly moustaches.

Sisyphus—haha, totally him. He'd run this store day in, day out since he was eighteen. That was eight whole years, and there'd be another eighty.

Nothing about that screamed Dead-End Dude.

'Journalist integrity'. Honestly, who wanted to keep dosing themselves into depression? It was to everyone's benefit that his magazines focused on practical matters—farming, horsing, gardening, food, fashion, fun. This was him *protecting*—top Capricorn trait—his fellow Earnest Pointers.

Also, not only did he have job stability and was his own boss, he had friends and family. He drank occasionally with beer buddies, regularly visited his aunt who posed as his mum, and bonded with his mum who pretended to be his cousin. Wasn't that some crazy-sounding roundabout? Dead-End Dude. "Absolute rubbish."

"What's rubbish?"

Carl lifted his head to his cousin (his real mum who didn't know he knew that and wouldn't ever as far as he was concerned) rushing towards him in a whirl of colour and lipstick. The smooch smacked the dimple of his grin, and she snatched the mag out of his hands.

"Ohh, this part sounds promising. 'Single Capricorns might have an increased desire for a permanent, fully committed relationship'." She dropped the mag on the counter and her gaze veered left. A sparkle hit her eye. "What's with the doghouse next to the counter here? Why does it have a big, floppy bow on it?"

Carl smirked. That was another thing. He not only had this store, friends and family, he had a *boyfriend*.

He moved to the kennel, patted the top of the fake-ceramic-tiled roof, and pointed inside. "My future."

"Is in the doghouse?"

"Yeah." He grinned and waved her in to see how awesome it all looked.

She came back out bouncing on her heels and gave him their special high-five-flick. "That's way cooler than a velvet box."

Carl threaded his fingers through his hair. "I want to surprise Pete when he finally gets back from uni this afternoon. It's been too long, this distance schtick. I'm ready for settling. He mentioned not being sure about where he'd stay last week—this solves that. He can move in with me."

"Ohmygod," she yelped and threw her arms around his neck, and then she yelped again, jerking a finger towards the sliding doors. Pete—fresh off the bus in casual jeans and geeky t-shirt—was trundling a suitcase towards the store. "I'll flip the sign to closed on my way out!"

She left with a dazzling hello to Pete, and Pete gave her a toothy smile and a hello back. Carl had been seeing that smile since they were three and got into mischief at kindergarten, and twenty-three years later, he still couldn't get enough of it.

He leapt over the counter, not caring he sent the mag slithering to the floor in his enthusiasm, and engulfed Pete in a fierce hug of flannel. He stepped back, rubbing Pete's upper arms as he took him all in. A little thinner than usual, and his gaze looked tired, lacking its usual glitter. "You eating enough?"

"It's been busy. Especially this last semester."

Explained why he'd called less and less. Carl wagged a finger at him, but he was the kind of guy who understood boundaries, people having stresses and needing space. It was okay that Pete had focused more on his studies.

"Let me take your suitcase—" Carl reached for it, but Pete stood it at his side.

"It's all good." Pete glanced at the kennel behind Carl. "What's this?"

A rush of nerves exploded in Carl's stomach; he rubbed his damp palms over the back of his jeans and sunk his fingers into the pockets. He nicked his head for Pete to come closer, and Pete took a few steps with a slight frown regarding the bow.

"We always said we'd get a dog someday," Carl said after clearing a lump in his throat. "I thought, now you're moving back, we could start on that soon? Ah, have a look inside."

Pete stared at the kennel, unmoving, and dropped his chin to his chest. Carl zipped to his side. "What's up?" He tucked a finger under Pete's chin and raised his head. Shimmery tears filled Pete's eyes. Carl never did tears himself but the sight of them had his heart pounding. He hauled Pete into a hug. "Hey, hey. I've got ya."

Pete shook his head against Carl's shoulder before resting it, catching his breath, and pulling out of his arms. "You're my best friend. You're really important to me. So this is hard."

"What's wrong? I'll help."

Pete met his gaze, his shadowed and wet. "Things have been different since I went to uni."

"Sure. It's been bloody hard work for you!"

"I meant . . . us. The boyfriending."

"Well, long distance. We can make it easier from now on." Carl gestured towards the kennel and Pete grabbed his extended arm and squeezed it.

"I don't want to."

Carl's ears pounded. He wasn't quite sure he'd heard that right. Before he could ask for a repeat, Pete continued. "Being apart made me realise. We're not really in love—wait, let me finish. I know we love each other, but it's like . . . family."

Carl didn't need clarification now. He rocked back on his heels. His gut felt like it was punched up his throat and might come out if he opened his mouth, so he kept it shut.

"We're better as friends. Best friends."

Carl nodded and nodded. He shoved a trembling hand through his hair and hoped his voice didn't catch. "Is there someone?"

Pete let out a long, slow breath.

"There is. —Not like that. I haven't acted on any of those feelings."

"But you have feelings."

Pete stepped forward and Carl did his best to stand still, not step back. He swallowed it all down.

"That's how I know what we have isn't love. Not passionate, romantic love."

Carl scratched the back of his head and stepped to the side, between Pete and his stupid proposal. Got this one wildly wrong. "Is that right?"

"I'm sorry."

"I mean . . . what's he like?" His throat tightened as he forced a laugh. "He'd better be good for my . . . best friend."

"We don't have to do this—"

"No, no. Let's. Get it all out now so I can process it all at once. Is he very different?"

Pete looked towards the journalistic-integrity-free magazine stand. "He's a mature student, like me. Started vet school after travelling the world. He's super fond of animals and got top marks in all his subjects; he tutored me in farm practical training, especially the agrichemicals modules . . ."

Pete got lost in admiring details of talented Nick, and Carl kept running his hand through his hair and nodding as his store suddenly came into sharp focus around him. This is what *his* life and future looked like. Hot pies, magazines, pet products, and emergency eggs.

"He has to do a six-month placement at a rural practice, and since we got on so well, he applied to one in Earnest Point."

"You're . . . moving in together?"

"I haven't told him my feelings yet, I needed to talk to you first. But I think he knows. Or he's . . . aware. He'd treat me well, Carl."

"Right." Nick could offer free medical care for their hypothetical dog for its hypothetical long life. Carl could offer a kennel. "Right."

Dead-End Dude.

He scrolled a hand through his hair again, nodding and nodding. Even forced out his dimples. "Right. Yeah. Sounds like he's a better fit. I'm curious to meet him."

Pete smiled dreamily, and it hit Carl like a storm. He could barely hold on.

This is what it felt like to be dashed to pieces.

[Dorothy] felt quite lonely, and the wind shrieked so loudly all about her that she nearly became deaf.

L. Frank Baum

The Wonderful Wizard of Oz

Chapter Two

At a half-broken bench on an outcrop overlooking Wellington, Carl cracked open the six-pack in his bag and drank while the city came to light-speckled life under a cold, misty night sky.

His hands numbed quickly, and he wished the rest of him would numb too. The stuff inside his chest kept twisting and turning, roaring. He could never go back. Never go back to being Carl Birch, dud, with no prospects and a penchant for accumulating fines.

After his sixth beer, cans squashed and stuffed back into his bag, he stood, shoved his flannel hoodie hood up over his head, and let the wind at his back push him to the edge of the bushy drop below. Over the sound of crunching gravel on the path behind him, he sighed, and the sigh fogged before him like a new path unfurling.

He opened his arms wide. Wellington. This new place, much bigger than Earnest Point, where no one knew Carl; this new place, where he didn't have to be Pete's best man; this new place . . . could he start over?

"Don't jump."

The voice was deep and calm, and totally unexpected. Carl whirled around, dizzy, pulse singing. A grey-hooded figure—washed in moonlight, vaguely shimmering in the moist air—strode his way. Power, urgency, determination radiated from him, and each of his steps was a curious punch to Carl's stomach. Seriously, the only thing missing from this moment was some kind of cape—

A ticklish laugh bubbled out, and—

Gravity raced through him.

Carl wasn't the type to topple over at the barest outline of a sexy man, but . . . He tried to catch himself, but his foot twisted and everything became a rush of sounds. Shouts—his own. Someone else's. His hand was suddenly burning where he'd grabbed hold of a branch and clung onto it while his feet scrabbled on prickly bushes to propel himself back up to the outcrop.

He wanted to start over, not reincarnate! He liked this body, this face; those could stay the same please-and-thankyou! Just the substance was the problem.

Arms extended towards him, strong hands curling around his upper arms. A flash of pinched brow overhanging the cliff, the mist making the world blurrier, the grunted, "Hold on. I've got you." And later, the desperate, "*I've got you this time.*"

A combination of Carl's own attempts and the stranger's heaving had Carl clambering over the precipice, and—

A final yank, the push of his foot finding purchase on a branch, throttling him forward against his saviour. They fell in a thumping heap to the firm, flat ground. For a good dozen seconds, Carl's heart hammered, adrenalin momentarily cleaving through the alcohol. A body was trapped under him. Firm lines, masculine, and breathing hard. A gruff, "Are you okay?"

"Yeah, mate. Thanks." Carl rolled to the side; his saviour sucked in air and began picking himself up, knocking Carl's bag from the bench in the process. A crushed can slipped out of the open zipper and was picked up again as Carl decided against standing until his head stopped spinning. God, it was spinning.

He blinked through it and took in his hero. The guy was tall, and the hood of his windbreaker was pulled up. His mouth and nose were covered by a scarf. A sparkly silver scarf. Carl couldn't tell if the shades of grey made some kind of pattern, like birds or fish or . . . wow. Even drunk, even with most of that face covered, Carl could tell the guy was curling a lip at him, unimpressed.

Alongside the unimpressedness, Carl made out dark eyes. Eyes that scrolled over his every inch unflinchingly. Eyes that pinched with apprehension. Eyes that *grimaced*.

"Drinking? While hiking on your own? At night? Are you an idiot?"

Eyes that saw the truth. This probably wasn't Carl's smartest idea. "Carrying on like a right pork chop, wasn't I?"

His saviour stuffed the can into his bag and zipped it up for him, muttering something about tourists. "Alright. Let's get you off this hill."

Carl waved a hand. He'd embarrassed himself enough. "I'm not that far gone. I can make it down on my own."

When his rescuer's dark gaze slunk up and down him again, Carl pushed through an ill-timed and ridiculously slinky shiver and got to his feet. "See?" He flung his bag over his shoulder, saluted Silver Scarf, and—with as much grace and dignity as he could muster in his state—marched past him to the dirt track and steep decline. *Grace* was a joke. As soon as he was out of sight, his movements turned to hobbles, and each hobble had his head pounding and his limbs sluggish.

At a particularly rocky bend, he stumbled and yelped.

He was rubbing his ankle when his silver-scarved hero raced in a scurry of dust to his side. By the light of his phone he checked Carl's ankle. Fingerless gloves thinly covered his hands and each press around Carl's foot was a bite of cold with the gentle scrape of blunt nails and the coarse kiss of wool. Carl's pant leg was pushed back down over the tender muscle. Dark eyes hit Carl again. "Looks okay, but to be sure, hop on my back."

"I'm sure I'll be—" Carl slipped again trying to stand. "Yep, sounds good."

A huff. Perhaps one that came with a grin? Hard to tell now Carl was staring at the man's broad back. A silly laugh twisted through him as he pressed himself against this silver saviour. Sharp plunging insides robbed Carl of any more laughter as his hero swiftly stood. Confident hands grabbed Carl's thighs and wrangled him higher up around slim hips.

"I'll get you down safe."

It took a moment to talk over the . . . giddiness. *Alcohol* induced. "Big heart you have, mate."

"Not heart. Social responsibility."

"Bet it weighs heavily on you."

A huffed laugh. Carl draped himself more closely to his saviour's back and closed his eyes against a firm, sturdy shoulder for the fifteen-minute piggy-back ride.

"You're strong."

"You're lucky. People are lining up for such a chance."

"To ride you?"

Silver-Scarf *tsk*ed; hands shifted down the undersides of Carl's thighs to his knees and jolted him up another two inches. The sudden friction had Carl hurriedly changing the topic.

"Anyway, what were *you* doing hiking in the dark?" He smirked. "Are you also an idiot?"

"People need to be more careful, that's what I meant. I shouldn't have called you an idiot."

Carl sighed. "It's okay, I was a bit."

"If you'd had an accident—if you'd fallen back there—

think of all the people who'd be hurt. Heartbroken. Look out for yourself, that's all. For you, and for them."

"You sound . . ." Carl lifted his head from one shoulder and laid it on the other. "Are *you* heartbroken?"

His saviour paused in his step for a moment before continuing, ignoring the question.

"I'm asking because you're taking this social responsibility very seriously."

"Would you rather I'd left you dangling from a cliff?"

Carl chuckled, but the kind of chuckle that preceded a groan. A groan that he expelled after he was deposited on a bus-stop bench.

His hero stuffed a red bus card into his hand, pivoted on his grey boots and disappeared.

Carl didn't actually need the bus to get home—his brother's place was literally two minutes up the road—but he was too tired to slur any of that. Instead, he called after his saviour's shadow, "Big heart. Yup. Owe you one."

After catching his breath—from the extremely exhausting effort of being carried down the hill—Carl crawled back to Jason's pad, a villa on a quarter-acre patch with heaps of lavender. He took a breather on the porch chair, and then fell into the spacious, pristine house.

The hallway was a good glimpse at the differences between him and his brother. They might be twins—with the same medium height, blue eyes, snobbish upturned nose, and dimpled smile—might both have this tiny freckle at their jaw, and even the same weird double-jointed toe. But that's where the similarities ended.

Just look at this hallway. Covered in framed, gleaming music awards, starting twenty years ago and carrying on throughout Jason's entire childhood and into adultdom. He was famous, in certain circles. Accomplished. Had a career that let him travel the world. Played for huge audiences. Was applauded by them.

Rubbing his nape, laughing, Carl stumbled to the grand piano in the living area and slumped onto the stool. The stand was crowded with heaps of notes—some Schulhoff concerto thing—and amongst the loose pages was a mag that Carl could actually read.

He'd read Jason's horoscope out to him before he'd left to play Carl back in Oz, but he'd skipped over his own in an effort to keep himself together. Now he was half undone anyway, so . . .

He snapped up the glossy paper and schlepped it to the master bedroom, where he stripped out of his beloved flannel and flopped into bed.

He flipped to the right page, and read . . . and tossed the mag aside, wagging a finger at it. "No integrity at all!"

~

The next morning, Carl's head was pounding. Like, really pounding.

It was hard to know, though, if it was due to the beer last night or the million thoughts that plagued him since reading his darned horoscope.

> Capricorn may have mistaken friendship for something more and bitterly resent himself for not seeing the signs, but rest assured, it's better to face the music. New relationships will reveal themselves as you grow from this experience in heart, mind, and courageous spirit!

Carl lifted one of the dozen pillows he'd drowned in last night and muffled a growl into its feathery mass. As if predestined or something, his phone shrilled with a call from his twin.

Jason sounded rather breathless as he interrogated Carl about the cop he shared a fence with back home. "I got the feeling you're rather infamous at the station."

"Well," Carl grimaced. "I might've been the subject of a tweet or two . . ."

Carl answered Jason's questions about his neighbour the sergeant on automatic, his mind blasting 'Dead-End Dude' like it was a chorus in a bad song. ". . . he seems as annoyed as I am that I'm always getting tickets. Or getting caught with a beer in a public place—" *Like last night*! "You know . . . I might have a problem with rules."

Carl should make it his mission: No more trouble.

But trouble, it seemed, was also plaguing his otherwise-rule-abiding twin brother who was currently at Carl's house pretending to be Carl. Turns out, pretending to be someone who looked exactly like you could actually be a bit tricky. Carl's grip on his phone doubled. This couldn't be all over before it began. He couldn't *face the music*. Pete, the boy he'd known forever. The one he'd been most comfortable with in the world. Pete, who was tying the knot with Nick. He had no guts to go back to Tas until the wedding. Even then . . . could he not run away forever?

When Jason vowed "This is not over yet," Carl let out a deep breath of relief.

Call over, he rolled out of bed, foot miraculously okay, and found Jason's bike and rainbow helmet in the garden shed. He always felt better leaving his devices behind and getting some good wind in his face, so he peddled hard and fast down the wide road towards Island Bay and swung a left around the coast. The surfers were out at Houghton Bay this morning, the sea sparkling turquoise and navy before crashing into white rushes up the beach, and it looked . . . like a good spot for a fast dip.

His shorts were pretty much the same material as swim shorts. They'd do.

He stripped off his flannel and the t-shirt under it, and stuffed his socks into his shoes. His stuff he left with the bike, leaning near some benches on the footpath.

He got as far into the—*crikey*—cold water as his hips when a familiar holler of boredom and mischief had him whirling towards the shore.

Just his luck. "Oi!"

His shout fell on dismissive ears; the rascals took off with his bike, one riding, the other perched on the bag rack.

A nearby surfer, already half stripped out of his soaked wetsuit at the back of his ute, caught the whole incident and sprinted—barefoot and bare chested—after the teens. He yelled . . . something. Whatever it was, it had the teens coming off the bike, abandoning it at the side of the road, and running off.

Carl waded out of the water and sand clung ticklishly to his feet and ankles. The surfer strode along the footpath, the bike alongside him. Grey neoprene clung low on his hips, the fine tight muscles on his perfectly tapered torso shifting under his damp skin. He moved with a cool, easy gait, showing off an overall physique that could only be described as . . . too much work.

Too much work and too hard to look away from. How many innocent bystanders got locked into gym memberships after looking at this?

Carl ignored an appreciative swoop in his belly and grinned as he came up the steps; his bike rescuer leaned the bike in its original spot, and then shook his dark, damp hair like he was being filmed for a shampoo advertisement. Like he *knew* he'd sell a lot of it.

When he glanced over at Carl, he did a double take and blinked. Carl totally got it; one of them was a heart-throb, and the other was a guy in sort-of-swimshorts too au-natural in colour. Possibly like he wasn't wearing anything. Upon closer inspection, though, things were all squared neatly away, everyone's purity preserved.

"Thanks."

Bike-Rescuing-Surf-Dude cocked his head, dark eyes stomach-jumpingly riveted onto Carl.

"You haven't seen a multicoloured helmet, have you? Or my clothes? Little devils."

Bike-Rescuing-Surf-Dude's frown deepened. He shook his head as if ridding himself of a wayward thought. "They took off with the helmet."

"What'd you say to get them to leave the bike?"

"They rightly figured they'd be in bigger trouble if they kept going. I know their mums. Lock your bike up next time. Your helmet will show up somewhere, no doubt."

He went on his way, and Carl followed with a thought. A small-towner, everyone's-your-friend-and-neighbour kind of thought. "Are you heading through Berhampore? Can't ride without a life-saving headpiece, I spotted cops out this morning." Carl leaned in where his bike rescuer was stretching a muscular arm into the ute. He pulled out a towel and flung it around his neck. "I'm doing this thing where I try not to get into trouble."

Judgy laughter, muffled through the towel as he wiped his face.

Carl looked from his stolen bike to his wet shorts and grimaced. "As you see, it's going well. Can I pop my bike in the back?"

Bike-Rescuing-Surf-Dude reached back into the bed of the ute—and pulled out a bright red helmet and oversized, equally red jacket. He pressed them against Carl's chest. "You're set."

Carl blinked as his rescuer hopped into the driver's seat, and sighed, patting the vibrant headsaver. "Toto, I've a feeling we're not in small-town Tassie anymore." He called out louder, "Where do I return these?"

A hand popped out of the open window and flashed a wave. And, with a roar of the engine, the ute peeled away from the curb.

CARL DONNED THE JACKET AND TOTO, FOUND ONE OF HIS shoes, and made do. At least the jacket was warm. And it smelled *good*—the pleasantest trace of aftershave lingered at the collar, and he kept breathing it in. The helmet was a perfect fit too, but he'd had to tighten the chin strap, which he'd perhaps done a little too tight, because it was rubbing under his jaw at his rather sensitive spot there . . .

He shook off the vision of the helmet's owner. Beautiful but a bit . . . aloof? Seriously, how much trouble would it have been to drive him? If this were Tassie . . .

He'd have bigger problems.

Carl screeched to a tire-burning halt as a crying strawberry-blond kid stepped blindly into the street.

The kid scrambled back with sorries and more tears, and Carl—well, tears really worried him. He stopped and asked if they were okay.

The kid looked panicked. "Bee sting."

"Oh shit," Carl said, frantically making a plan to flag the next passerby and get them to call for an ambulance. "You allergic?"

"N-no," they cried. "It just hurts. I want to go home but I don't want the other kids to see me. Boys sh-shouldn't c-cry."

"Aw, kiddo. Boys can cry whenever they like! Where d'you live?"

"B-berhampore."

Thirty-minute walk. Or five minutes on the back of Carl's

bike. He took Toto the Red Helmet off and set it on the boy. "Hop on, I'll get you home quick."

The boy hopped onto the bag rack and clung to Carl all the way, then thanked him and streaked towards his house with the helmet on. At the same moment, a cop unfolded from a car across the road and trundled towards him. Carl knew from experience what that grimace-and-swagger meant. He bowed his head and gritted his teeth. Riding without a helmet. Another ticket.

So much for avoiding trouble.

He was on his way again, pushing his bike up the hill, when someone called from behind him. He turned to a young woman with bright strawberry blond hair and guessed at a glance she was related to the boy; if he hadn't been certain from the hair, the red helmet she carried would've clued him in.

"Thank you for helping Leo home." She tapped Toto and gestured to his red jacket. "You're not from Over The Raindough."

Over The Raindough. Is that where Bike-Rescuing-Surf-Dude worked?

"How do you know I don't work there?"

She laughed and pointed diagonally across the road to a bright red bakery façade he hadn't noticed. "*I* work there."

Really? "Do you know a tall guy there?" Carl asked her after a short explanation how he ended up in half of the delivery uniform and how he'd come to help *Leo*—her son, she said—home. He took Toto when she handed it back to him. "Around my age? Surfer type?"

She smiled brightly. "Ah, you mean Berhampore's heart-breaker. You don't get out much. He's working the early shift tomorrow."

Heartbreaker? Beautiful and probably knew it, a little aloof . . . That fit. "Heartbreaker, eh?"

She giggled. "You'll see."

"I just want to return these when I'm done with them."

"That's what they all say."

"Muuuuum!" Leo yelled from behind the fence. "You left the stove on, and this jam isn't helping."

Carl chuckled. "He means honey, right? Onion helps too."

"Honey! I knew it was one or the other." She started running back to Leo, frantically apologising. "Head full of straw, I have."

Carl waved, and Leo's young mum shut her gate and whirled back, yelling. "By the way, there's another reason I know you don't work at Over The Raindough."

"What's that?" A bakery would totally be the type of job Carl would gravitate towards.

"You're Jason Lyall, right? Piano genius? The one all the mums want their sons to turn out like?"

Jason. Genius.

Carl sighed and dropped his head, which might have looked like a nod because it received a delighted squeal. "I *knew* it. From the pics they posted of your latest concert-album."

"Oh wait—"

She clapped her hands as Leo pulled at her elbow to remind her that he was there and he still had an ouchy. She stepped back, staring at Carl with big, awed eyes. And those eyes. Not gonna lie. They tickled his pulse. To be looked at like that. Adored. It was a pleasant kind of feeling. Quite addictive, he could imagine.

"Please, please," she said. "We have our Street Greet tomorrow evening, the mums will be *amazed* if I got you to come. Would you?"

Of course he wouldn't.

Would he?

Early the following morning, Carl was still debating this. He shook his wet hair, fresh from a shower, and opened Jason's wardrobe. A couple of lonely shelves in the corner held all his comfy jeans, soft t-shirts, and the softer flannel that he liked to throw over them. The rest of the space was filled with pressed suits, coats with long tails, casual-fancy blazers, skinny jeans and skinnier t-shirts.

Jeez. Yeah, even the wardrobe looked accomplished.

He picked out a button-up shirt, a tie, and a waistcoat which shared a hanger with the matching pants. He held up the shirt against his damp chest. Good thing about this twin business. All this would fit.

What if . . . what if—until he headed back home—he pretended he *was* successful? *He* had this dreamy villa, these fancy suits, expensive wines. The grand piano and the manicured backyard. He could *be* Jason while Jason was being Carl. Carl was good at the Kiwi accent, too. He could totally pull it off. Live as if all this were really his.

Carl shook his head violently and stuffed the outfit away. Silliness. Jason posing as Carl in the lead-up to his ex's wedding was understandable. It addressed Carl's broken heart and gave Jason the chance to meet his biological family. Play-acting to make himself feel like he had a bright future—a bright *present* —full of big boulevards and no dead ends . . . might be indulging himself a bit.

He stuffed on his own jeans and his flannel hoodie, grabbed the red jacket and Toto, and emerged into a dark, dewy morning. It was five a.m., and honestly, Carl loved being up this early. In Aussie he was up at four-thirty most mornings. Nothing compared to the quiet that came with this time. The freshness of the air. The first calls of birds.

He followed still-bright lampposts down to the shops and Over The Raindough, the only building glowing with life.

He rapped against the door and peered through the glass. The form of a figure came around a counter, but was obscured by the partially fogged glass, and—

The door snicked and whooshed open. His bike saviour, in charcoal jeans, a grey t-shirt, and—most prominently—a flour-dusted apron the colour and shine of tinfoil. Dark hair sat behind a dark net, and darker eyes glinted under short lashes. The corner of his mouth twitched as if in spite of itself. "No Trouble Boy." He looked at all the red Carl carried. "Easy enough to find me?"

"It was . . . no trouble." Carl winced.

Berhampore's-Supposed-Heartbreaker-and-Carl's-Bike-Rescuer folded his arms. "What prompted a pre-dawn delivery?"

There was something about the way he said it that implied Carl was acting like a love-struck stalker. Like he'd felt the echo of the sharp, low shiver Carl experienced upon seeing him. Well, the guy could get that idea out of his mind asap! Those shivers were out of his control. Physical only. Automatic response.

There was only one reason he was here. "Like they say. The early bird—" Carl went to set the bundle on the table inside to avoid all that dusty flour—and be done with the visit—but his foot hit the raised threshold and he tripped violently, tackling his rescuer to the floor. Whoosh, another few bolts of out-of-his-control electricity. The helmet and jacket flew across the timber boards and they ended up a sprawled tangle of limbs. Both expelled shocked puffs of air; Carl slammed his eyes shut as he peeled his cheek off his rescuer's groin. "—catches the worm," he finished on a mortified whimper.

His rescuer let out a short, sharp laugh at this, and tried to sit up as Carl attempted to extricate himself—

Their foreheads met with a resounding smack, and they

toppled back to the floor, lips parting—and clashing—as they groaned . . .

They froze, suspended in the shock of tingling skin and the drizzle of released breath. Dark eyes hit Carl's and the long limbs under him shifted.

There were freckles at the edges of his eyes, making his short lashes appear thicker. The arch of his brow. Something about this felt *familiar* . . .

A hand pressed against Carl's chest, and finally, finally Carl ripped their mouths apart and threw himself aside. "That threshold is hazardous."

"Sure it's the threshold?"

Before arriving here, Carl had imagined asking the guy's name and suggesting a drink to thank him for the bike rescue, but he quickly dismissed that idea. Especially after he'd gone and mauled the stranger. The last thing he wanted was for any of this to be misconstrued. This was *not* Carl trying his luck!

He jumped to his feet, gathered and plunked all the red on a table, thanked the man for his services—headpalm—and dove out of Over The Raindough with no intention of ever returning. He could bake his own bread, thanks. Ice his own cupcakes.

No need to see those dark, gently judgy eyes ever again.

You must walk. It is a long journey, through a country that is sometimes pleasant and sometimes dark and terrible.

L. Frank Baum

The Wonderful Wizard of Oz

Chapter Three

He saw those dark, gently judgy eyes again that very day.

The first time, at the roundabout. Carl had stopped abruptly at the sight of Jason's rainbow helmet hanging from the powerlines, and a vehicle had to come to a sudden halt. This had Carl jumping and throwing out a thanks that got truncated when he noticed the familiar ute, and the more familiar dark-haired heartbreaker behind the wheel. The toot that came sounded incredulous, and their eyes locked as the ute carefully passed.

The second time, after lunch. Carl had headed off to explore Jason's suburb on foot, and narrowly avoided being run down by an electric scooter. In the process of leaping aside, he smacked his hand on a freshly painted green fence, through the gaps of which dark eyes stared with a series of disbelieving blinks. Carl blinked back, and Berhampore's Heartbreaker rose out of his crouch with his green-dripping paintbrush, reached over the pickets, and without a word erased Carl's handprint.

The third time, mid-afternoon, when Carl headed to the supermarket to stock the pantry and ended up on the phone with Jason, shaking his head at his twin becoming involved in a fake-boyfriend plot in his name—only to have Berhampore's Heartbreaker round into his aisle as he was saying ". . . I'm into PDA." Which earned him a look like Carl had said it only to let *him* know. Like he really was hounding after him!

He returned home, unpacked, dealt with a wash he'd forgotten to hang out, and slunk into a local bar to drown the mortifying moments involving those gently judgy eyes. Seriously, who *was* this guy?

Behind the bar, the bartender was unpacking a box of cider. Carl used the time to glance over the beer list.

"What would you like?"

"A hazy IP—" Carl looked up and lost the rest of his order. His mouth gaped open, and unfortunately, he suspected a string of saliva had followed in the suddenness—leading to yet another assumption Carl was here drooling at all this beauty.

There—that jump of his brow. That totally implied he thought Carl was another groupie chasing after him.

Outrageous.

He smacked away any traces of unwanted drool. "*Just the beer*, please."

He paid, zipped to the furthest table available, and shielded himself from view with a menu. His beer came with a low tutting and blunt-tipped fingers dragging condensation off the glass. Carl refused to look up until he was sure the man was once more behind the bar.

Yep, stay right there where he could keep an eye on him, make sure he didn't *poof!* and turn up again in Carl's shadow.

A gaggle of prettily dressed-up ladies and gents swelled into the pub and took seats at the bar. Carl wanted to point a finger and declare *that* was flirting, nothing like what he'd done. He shook his head and grumbled into his beer. And grumbled some more upon witnessing those groupies getting sweet, polite smiles.

Not that he was a groupie, dammit.

At the table behind a beam on his right, Carl caught a glimpse of three middle-aged women in various shades of green seating themselves and clinking their wine glasses. "Let's down these, girls, and head to the Street Greet."

The Street Greet. He'd forgotten about it. Which was probably an indication he'd sensibly given up the thought of heading there as his twin.

"I saw Sage when I picked up some breadsticks," one of them said. "She was harking on about having seen Jason Lyall; she's invited him, apparently."

"Probably meant she glimpsed him heading home and stuffed a flyer in his letterbox. She's always exaggerating."

"She has to, though. She's got nothing else to talk about."

"Bit dim, that one."

"What kind of conversation do you expect from a mum who got knocked up at fifteen?"

"All right, fair. We can all just nod and smile."

"It's the kind thing to do. Won't last long anyway, she can't keep up with other things."

"So do we ask about Jason?"

A scoff. "Don't be so mean. You know he never takes part in these things. There's no way he'd show up."

"Honestly. *Sage.* How'd she end up with a name like that?"

"She's a baker. It still fits."

Laughter.

Carl's stomach twisted.

The out-of-towner and his magazines. His ex marrying super-smart veterinarian Nick. A corner store stockpiling donuts and kitty Catbernet. Duds and dead ends.

These women laughing at Sage behind her back could have been laughing at him.

He abandoned the last of his beer, pulled up his flannel hood, sidled past the groupies, and balled his fists the entire way to the villa. There, in a haze of sympathy and self-pity, he yanked open Jason's wardrobe.

CARL TOOK HIS CLEANLY SHAVEN JAWLINE AND STYLED HAIR towards Sage's Street Greet, dressed in a perfectly tailored charcoal suit. A glance in a shop window had him squaring his shoulders with confidence. The charcoal, the crisp white, the black tie. Sharp. He totally exuded *accomplished.*

But . . . jeez, it was a wee bit constricting.

The jacket was the problem. Sort of pinched around his biceps. Perhaps he could get away without it? The double-breasted waistcoat should still give off a slick air of the refined.

On the main drag, before turning into the Street Greet, he shrugged out of the jacket and a typical Wellington gust made off with it. He attempted to play chase, but there came the blur of bike wheels and all that tailored material cling-wrapped the rider, who swore under wool and silk.

Carl watched between his fingers as the helmeted figure continued riding, one hand pulling the jacket off and holding it by its collar. Yeah, that grip wasn't lessening. Yup, the rider was taking off with it.

Looked like Carl would be replacing that one.

Never mind. The Street Greet . . .

He turned the corner and headed towards the end of the road. Like he'd stepped into some kind of alternate universe, evening sunset streamed down on him in glorious gold as he walked towards the gathered residents and their jaw-dropped mouths.

"Is that Jason Lyall?"

"The musician?"

"Oh my God. I go to all his local shows."

"Ha, I go to the ones in Auckland too."

"I need his autograph!"

"I want to hear him play."

"I wonder what his favourite pieces are!"

"Those fingers!"

"Truly talented."

Did they call him 'truly talented'?

Wow, were they actually scrambling to make way for him?

"He usually keeps to himself."

"Who lured him out?"

"Does he know Sage? Are they . . .?"

"No way she could know someone like him."

Carl spotted Sage at the far end, on the edge of the crowd, her strawberry head cast down as if she'd caught all that too. She was starting to slink away.

"Sage!" Carl called out, and waltzed past the three bit —*witches*—from the pub. "Nice to see you again. How's Leo?"

Sage looked up, blossoming into a smile. And gosh, how satisfying, seeing the mums sag into mystified puddles as he accepted Sage's wide-armed, bouncy "Hello!"

Being Jason Lyall was rather intoxicating.

He smiled at neighbours and signed Jason's name on t-shirts and notebooks and promised to help a few old ladies tune their pianos. Really, he couldn't say no, could he? He'd simply put it off until the real Jason returned. He'd tell his brother helping out was good for karma.

He let Sage introduce him to everyone, and when asked by one of the witches to remind them of the story behind Tartini's *Devil's Trill Sonata* he begged off to 'visit the bathroom.'

Sage ushered him to her place, calling into the house for Leo to come out. "Grayson is bringing your favourite apple shortcake! Made from the apples off our tree!"

When there was no response, Sage 'huh'ed. "Maybe he's already found him. I'll go check." And Carl was left to find the toilet on his own.

Not that he needed it. But he went in anyway and perched on the fluffy lid while frantically searching up musical histories.

On his way back out, he caught sight of Leo peering out from under the table. "Psst."

Carl checked he wasn't talking to anyone behind him and pointed to himself. At Leo's nod, he crouched and waited.

Leo whispered, "Are they out there?"

"The neighbours? Yeah."

"The other mums?"

Carl nodded again.

Leo shuddered. "I'll stay here, then."

Carl thought of the ones he'd met so far, and had to agree. "What about that apple shortcake?"

"This is a conundrum!"

Carl laughed. "How about I sneak some in for you?"

"You'll come back?"

Carl winced, imagining all the other musical queries that'd come his way. "Fairly sure I'll be hiding in the bathroom again soon."

"I'm good at hiding. I can show you some better spots!" Leo brightened and crawled out from under the table. "First find Grayson. His shortcake is the best. The other mums try to make it but theirs is too sour."

"Grayson's shortcake. Got it." Carl rose to his feet; only after he closed Sage and Leo's gate did he wonder: who was this Grayson? What was he supposed to look like?

He didn't spy Sage, but one of the friendlier older ladies—Linda?—whose piano he'd promised to tune smiled and beckoned him to a picnic table on the footpath. "You look lost."

"Need to find someone."

"Of course you do, honey."

Carl scratched the back of his head. "His name's Grayson?"

"Nice young man. Bit burdened by his past."

That was . . . a bit more information than he needed. "Any idea where to find him?"

"It'll be quite a journey."

"He lives very far from here? Any idea when he'll arrive?"

"You'll find one another eventually."

Sage returned with a chipper laugh and a hug for Linda. She patted the top of Linda's white ringlets, and mouthed to Carl that she wasn't all there.

That was . . . quite okay.

What wasn't okay was the sudden reappearance of the witches. "You're back. Where were we? Ah, *Devil's Trill Sonata*."

"Tell us about it."

"Yes! Please do."

Carl started to sweat under his double-breasted waistcoat and paused to channel his best Jason: Knowledgeable. Professional. Accomplished.

He wriggled his fingers. Giuseppe Tartine's Violin Sonata in G Minor. Often performed with a piano accompaniment. He cleared his throat and told them the story he'd just looked up online. "Guiseppe Tartine dreamt he made a pact with the devil: his soul in return for musical genius. After obliging, the devil took Giuseppe's violin and played the most enchanting sonata he'd ever listened to. Upon waking, Giuseppe rushed to put all he'd heard down on parchment. The trill was challenging for many a musician, and this sonata was full of them. So full, he named the tricky piece after the tricky devil who gave it to him. Devil's Trill."

"Fascinating! Are there many other stories about musical pieces?"

Carl tugged at his tie. "I wouldn't know where to begin."

"What about—" one of the witches started, and Carl jerked a finger towards the table, where a pitcher of lemonade and a stack of plastic cups sat.

"Excuse me," he rasped. "Throat's a bit sore. Talk more another time."

He dashed for the lemonade, and Linda helped pour it for him. Sage, perched on a chair beside her, cupped her chin and stared up at him in awe.

Carl felt a little guilty at this. But then he remembered how Sage had cheered up seeing Jason Lyall come to her Street Greet and nodded to himself. Right thing to do under the circumstances.

Sage waved brightly to someone behind Carl and to the left. "Grayson!"

Grayson of the apple shortcake?

Carl turned—and dropped his lemonade in a sticky splash down his waistcoat. *That was Jason's suit jacket!* And in it . . .

Gently-Judgy-Eyes.

They both blinked. Carl in an incredulous, you're-kidding-me way, and Grayson in an I-expected-nothing-less-from-my-newest-groupie way.

Grayson stared at him, a long scroll from silk tie to polished Oxfords. And those dark, judgy eyes were in fine form.

Which was . . . completely enraging. Such a thought must be stopped at once. "I'm not into you!"

"No one's introduced you?" Sage began pointing between them. "Grayson, Jason Lyall. Jason, Grayson Woods. Ha, that's a mouthful. Let me take that plate off you." She whisked the apple shortcake to the table, and in the process became a momentary buffer between them. Carl stepped back, shaking his head in utter disbelief, while two twenty-somethings in slinky black dresses came over and pulled Grayson in their direction.

One held out a small card to him. "This is to thank you for helping my aunt paint her fence."

"No problem," Grayson said with a polite smile.

"I—I'd like to take you out to dinner to say thank you?"

Grayson pocketed the card. "This is thanks enough." With that he walked away—towards Carl!—and paused as he passed, whispering with a scrape of lips against his ear, "by the way, that isn't how you pronounce Giuseppe."

Carl's heart did a wild, panicky lurch and set off a cascade of shivers.

Grayson had been watching him since *then*?

Carl had *pronounced the composer's name wrong*?

Oh shit.

Had that been what his judgy eyes were about?

Was the gig already up?

Carl spun around and watched the man disappear into Sage and Leo's home.

An arm hooked around his and Sage grinned up at him. "We all gaze after him like that."

Carl blinked at her. "What's his problem?"

"Why does he reject us all, you mean?" He actually meant in the metaphorical sense, but Sage kept going. "Not sure exactly. He doesn't talk about it, but he's been like that since his mother died and he broke up with his ex. Two years ago."

A loud crackle and squeal came from a megaphone, and a voice was amplified.

"A reminder number five, seven, nine, and eleven have opened their backyards for you all to admire their gardens."

Sage 'ohhhed' and jogged off, and at the sight of a witch pivoting in Carl's direction, Carl scooped up some apple shortcake in a napkin and made for Sage's—

Another witch came towards him, blocking that route—were they *triangulating* him? His only option was next door, number eleven with the open backyard.

Along the side of the house he went, only to emerge into a beautifully manicured garden where the third witch was greeting neighbours on the back deck.

She saw him, waved, and loudly asked her 'hubby' to help her bring out the electric keyboard.

Trapped.

Of course, he *could* confess to his crime, but . . . the entire neighbourhood would be laughing at Sage behind her back if he did.

They'd be laughing behind his back too.

He couldn't face it.

He started up the side of the house again and reversed upon glimpsing familiar green fabric rounding from the front yard. He jogged deeper into the garden, looking for a tree to hide behind, or—

Sage's place was next door.

He tucked the napkin-wrapped apple shortcake into his breast pocket.

At a distant cackling laugh, Carl rushed the fence, threw himself over it, and landed in . . . outstretched, charcoal grey arms.

It is such an uncomfortable feeling to know one is a fool.

L. Frank Baum

The Wonderful Wizard of Oz

Chapter Four

Carl was one rampant heartbeat. He'd vaulted the fence in a hurry, but he'd expected to land on leafy uneven ground. Not to roll his foot on an apple and topple into Grayson, who dropped a bushel of Braeburns to catch him.

Arms came tightly around his waist, fingers pressing in. A burst of breath scuttled over his left ear. One finger dug in close to his spine. There they teetered, on the cusp of a horizontal stumble—and Grayson shifted his feet, stabilising them. *Thank God.* The proximity, though . . . Chests and thighs jammed together, peculiarly warm against the cooler breeze around them, and their noses met with startling electrical currents.

Carl's eyes widened in shock and horror, and Grayson's sparked with a lift of an eyebrow.

"Not into me, eh?"

Oh my God. His life was seriously unbelievable.

He shoved out of Grayson's arms with a scowl, only to drop his gaze to Jason's jacket and come right back to peel it off him—

"You guys okay?" came a baffled voice beside them and Carl froze, hands half in Grayson's shirt.

This . . . might not look totally PG.

Carl freed his hands, pretending to dust the lapels instead.

He felt the rumble of Grayson's quiet laughter under his palms, and smartly turned to wide-eyed Leo. "Ah, I brought you something." He took out the slightly squashed apple shortcake and handed it over.

"Thanks?"

"No problem."

Leo blinked from him to Grayson to the fence and back to him. "You sure about that?"

Well . . .

From over the fence came the call of 'his' name. "Jason? Jason? Where did he go? The piano's waiting for him."

Carl shrank into a ball at Grayson's feet and started crawling towards Sage's house, curling a finger to Leo, whispering, "Where's that hiding place you mentioned?"

Grayson side-stepped in front and crouched to Carl's level with an expression of utter bewilderment and suspicion. Yet, the hand that met Carl's shoulder and steered him to sit back on his haunches was gentle, careful. A glimpse behind a tinny façade?

Grayson's tight-lipped inquisitive *grimace* brought Carl back from the stray thought. He smiled wanly. "Met my daily limit of social interaction. I'll just . . ." He started to crawl around Grayson and was stopped by gentle hands again, this time cupping his elbow and drawing him to his feet.

"Instead of hiding," Grayson said, keeping his voice low, "let's leave. I've got something for you."

"You can give the jacket back right here."

"I've got something *else* for you."

Something else? Like what, a few words of warning? An outright rejection of all Carl's supposed advances?

Carl wasn't exactly thrilled at this prospect either, but—

"*Find him, find him. It'd be so great if he could play Devil's Trill.*"

Carl held out his hands in surrender. "Take me far away from here."

He called out "See ya" to Leo, who was watching them curiously while nibbling on his shortcake, and then suddenly Carl was in the thick of the Street Greet. Neighbours crowded them, and Carl instinctively clutched Grayson's elbow as they pushed through the fray of eyelash flutters and constant questions.

"Are you not travelling to Europe to perform?"

Carl threw out the truth for once that evening. "Taking a few weeks holiday."

"Oh, excellent! Could you give a speech at the school assembly?"

"Oh, yes, please do! Always looking for inspirational speakers."

"I'll have to check my calendar." Carl knew now, it'd be very full of make-believe appointments. What could he talk about? He wasn't *actually* a musician. He'd get up, speak nonsense, and . . .

A whole assembly would applaud him.

Carl bit his lip. No. No way. Bad idea. Had this experience taught him nothing?

Grayson towed him through the Street Greet until they were rounding the corner towards the shops and freedom.

Carl trundled along, asking, "Weren't you working at the pub? It was you on the bike, who stole my jacket. I thought you had a ute?"

"If I've got the surfboard or work equipment, I take the ute. Otherwise, biking's the way to go. As for the pub, I was filling in. The boss was running late."

"What's your *actual* job?"

"Bit of everything."

That wouldn't help Carl determine how best to avoid him. He let go of Grayson's elbow. *In the future.*

Grayson opened the "Closed" Over the Raindough, and Carl made a point of lifting his foot over the high threshold as he crossed it. Now they were away from prying eyes, Carl decided one last try would be acceptable. After that, goodbye. Adios! Have a good life.

He crossed close to Grayson and with fast and furious fingers started wrangling off Jason's jacket, jerking his hands under the lapels and over firm shoulders—

Grayson snapped himself away, holding Carl back by a palm to his shoulder. "I hate to always be the heartbreaker, but—"

Heartbreaker?

Carl didn't hear the rest. He scrambled back with an incredulous laugh. "You can't break *my* heart. It's already broken!" Once Carl heard the words that'd flown out of his mouth he added hurriedly, "I mean, I'm not into you to begin with! That's my jacket."

Grayson buttoned back up with a mischievous gleam in his gaze. "It flew into my face. I might've fallen off my bike. The shock . . . Wearing this tonight seems like fair compensation."

In fact, Carl had been mightily relieved that jacket-flying thing *hadn't* caused an accident. It might've been quite serious. Best not push his luck too hard; he'd replace the jacket before Jason returned. With that matter sorted, he should extricate himself. "I'll be off then."

"Wait a moment."

Carl sighed and braced himself for the warning and/or misplaced rejection.

Instead, Grayson moved around the empty bakery counter and came back with his red helmet. "Here." He pressed it against Carl's chest. "This'll keep you safe. Stop you getting any more fines."

"Wait. How do you know I got fined?"

"Saw you helping Leo home yesterday. You didn't look thrilled to see that cop."

"You really are *everywhere*." Carl stepped towards him—instinctive curiosity. "What's your secret?"

Grayson stepped closer, a tickle of breath against Carl's cheek. "What's yours?"

Carl gave a fidgety-sounding laugh, heart racing rampantly. "What do you mean?" What *did* he mean? Did he . . . Had his terrible pronunciation of Giuseppe given him away? Or his unseemly cowering behind the fence?

Grayson watched him carefully. His look said *I've got my eye on you*.

Well, that was just . . . Carl prodded a finger into that firm chest. "You're always looking at me like that. Sure you aren't into me?"

Grayson rocked on his heels with a startled laugh. But before he could say something mildly scathing, the bakery door swung open and Sage wandered inside with a curious can-I-come-in smile.

"Saw you two take off. Neither of you have eaten."

Ideally, Carl would've bolted. But Sage experienced far too many people giving her excuses, and he didn't want to make her feel like she'd maybe done something wrong.

Smiling and nodding, he dragged out a chair and plunked himself into it. Grayson seated himself opposite, and Sage planted the plate she'd brought with her between them then hurried towards the kitchens. "Start with the sammies. This quiche is best warmed up."

Carl bounced his foot and bit into a sandwich, and calculated how many minutes before he could politely leave.

Grayson kept watching him. "We can talk, if you like."

"Ah, no. I'm good, thanks."

"You keep falling over me. We've felt each other in places reserved for third dates. What's the harm in sharing words?"

Carl snapped his eyes to Grayson's, trying not to recall the swoops each time those places had . . . met. "Fine. How many groupies do you have?"

"Sorry?"

"Girls and boys who fawn over you?"

Grayson leaned over the table with a curling lip. "Including or excluding you?"

Carl tossed his bread crust at him, and Grayson picked it up and ate it. "You should eat these."

"Why do you keep looking at me like that, all judgy?"

"You make me curious."

"*That's* curiosity?"

"Where are you from?" Grayson asked.

A bolt of panic shot through Carl's middle. "What?"

"Your accent confuses me. First it was very Aussie. Now it's . . . like you've watched a lot of Shortland Street."

Carl rang out a high-pitched laugh. "I . . . well . . . actually, if you must know, I've been practicing different accents. Additional to being a pianist, I dabble in voice acting."

An arched brow. "What have you narrated?"

Nothing. "Nothing you'd know. Sage!" He stood abruptly and moved towards her and a hot plate of quiche. "Let me help."

He shuttled the plate to the table while Sage thanked him—Jason Lyall—for coming along today. Carl stuffed a slice of quiche into his mouth and gave her two thumbs up. When it looked like Grayson might say something else, Carl picked up another quiche slice and popped it into his opening mouth. "Delicious. Try it."

While Grayson worked on the sudden mouthful, Carl wished Sage a lovely evening and—at the sight of Grayson's

Adam's apple bobbing and then his throat clearing—hurried a salute and made for the door.

Ah, the helmet!

He doubled back, grabbed it, and dashed out again.

Honestly, wasn't it enough to have seen Grayson five times earlier? Why did he have to show up at the Street Greet as well?

Best Carl avoided him.

Yes, best avoid them all. Can't have playing Jason get out of hand. He'd done his good deed for the day, enjoyed the thrill of being admired.

He'd stop now.

Carl avoided Berhampore the next morning, deciding to take his morning coffee habit to the neighbouring suburb of Newtown. It was quite strange not having to go to work, and he wasn't sure he loved the aimlessness of it. He'd better make a plan. See all the sights. Visit old school mates who'd settled here.

After a visit to the national museum, he met those old mates for lunch.

Turned out they were both lawyers and had each recently become engaged to the woman of their dreams.

Carl blinked in their spotless suits and slick smiles and tried not to shrink in his leather booth-seat. He spooned his pho and nodded along to all their adventure stories. "Probably head to Europe again later this year. Foodie tour around Georgia."

"We're doing Portugal."

Carl was doing nothing. "Nice. Nice."

"What about you?" one of them asked while he slurped up a noodle. "When was the last time you visited Tas?"

"Live there still, actually," Carl said.

"Really? Not little ol' Earnest Point, I hope!"

"Little ol' Earnest Point."

"What are you doing there? Can't be easy to grow your career. Where'd you go to uni in the end?"

Carl shook his head. "Didn't go."

The two lawyers made an 'ah' sound that felt like the beginning of the end of their meet up. "Trade school?"

Nope. "I work at the local convenience store."

"Wasn't that the part-time job you had at school?"

His stomach took a dive. "Running it now."

"With the bigger stores delivering, it's still keeping afloat?"

"We're quite remote. You'd be surprised how many locals love their daily donuts."

"Sure. Sure." Awkward silence followed.

The lawyers drank up the last of their phos, insisted they pay and he "keep his money", and took their leave, wishing him luck. Carl meandered back through the city towards Jason's, unable to shake off the feeling of pity they'd left him with. Like he'd revealed himself to be their high school's biggest disappointment and only luck might give him a better future. Like if he only had brains in his head he would be as good a man as any of them.

Carl ducked into a dairy, bought a mag, and tried to jostle up his spirits reading it at the nearby war memorial park.

Heads up, Capricorn, this week will be studded with surprises. . .

Carl laughed. Wasn't that true already?

He read on, stalling over the last part. *You'll meet three people this week. A Gemini in need. A Leo looking for luck. And a Scorpio specialising in stirring stuff up. You may be inclined to hide, but take a deep breath—you'll have to face them eventually.*

"You're meant to offer levity, not ominous foreboding."

Magazine stuffed into his bag, Carl schlepped through Newtown and up the incline towards Berhampore. He was cresting the hill when a swarm of yellow and green spilled onto the street and Carl took a seat on a low brick wall to avoid being flattened by scootering pre-teens.

When it seemed safe, he started up the footpath again, only to halt at the sight of Sage's Leo, wearing the same uniform as he'd watched pass him a hundred odd times, only his was . . . soaking wet. And his head was sunk to his chest.

Some bigger kids were snickering as they scurried around a corner; they looked suspiciously like the rascals who'd stolen his bike.

Badly behaving boys.

Carl jogged over to Leo, shrugged out of his flannel shirt, and gave it to the boy to keep him warm on the walk home. They were headed in the same direction, so Carl kept him company. He asked for Leo's star sign, was unsurprised to find him a Leo—but one couldn't assume these things—and went on to read him his weekly horoscope. "Things will pick up by the end of the week!"

"Doubt it," Leo said. "It's my week to help with assembly. Last week, Davy had his doctor dad come as a guest speaker, and he gave everyone ice-blocks full of electrolytes. No one I've asked can make it."

A Leo looking for luck.

Carl told himself off. Of course he couldn't . . .

Leo sniffed, and water those boys had dumped on him dripped from a curl onto his cheek and ran down like a tear.

Capricorn *was* ruled by Saturn, and Saturn was the planet of responsibility. And hadn't this become his social responsibility? Just like the sexy stranger who'd come to his rescue up at the outcrop. He'd been given a hand by fate. He should pay it forward.

Carl clapped a hand on Leo's shoulder. He'd worry about the details later. "Chin up. This famous pianist will be your guest speaker."

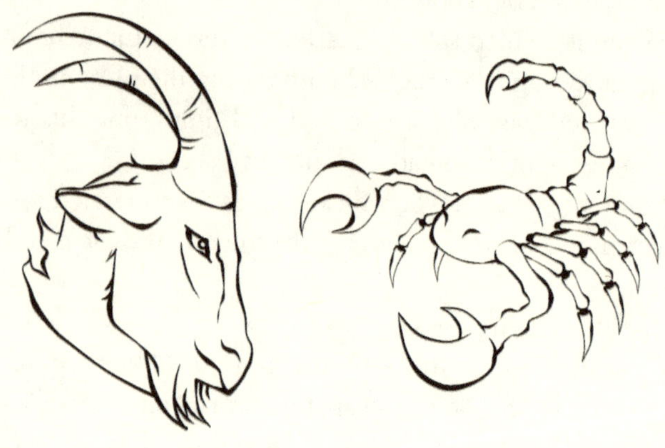

But after all brains are not the best things in the world.

L. Frank Baum

The Wonderful Wizard of Oz

Chapter Five

Carl had quite a few drinks that evening at the Berhampore local. He wasn't struck with inspiration how to pull off being a musical genius guest speaker, but he *was* struck with all-consuming laughter. The please-pity-me kind.

Guess who'd come to help out behind the bar?

He wagged a finger at Grayson. Shook his head. Drank another beer.

Twelve hours later he was preparing to nurse a headache by making a mid-morning smoothie. The night had become a blur.

He rubbed his temples.

Never mind that. More pressing was a plan for Leo's assembly—

His phone shrilled. A call. From the musician himself.

Carl spent the first few minutes of the call fretting alongside his double. Seemed like they were twins indeed, the way they gravitated towards trouble . . .

An obnoxiously loud whizzing sounded outside, and it did horrible things for his head. He gritted his teeth and pulled out essentials: banana, apple, yoghurt, berries . . .

Jason sighed down the line. "How're things for you in Wellington? Anything I need to know about? Post?"

Carl almost upended the blender. Um . . . He swallowed hard.

"Carl?"

He set the blender down with a thunk. "Oh, look at the time. I've gotta go. Later."

He hung up and tossed his phone onto the counter and paced the spacious room. The whizzing seemed to echo in the space, and he marched towards the worst of it, ending up in the master bedroom where the windows sat close to the chest-high fence separating the villa from the next yard. "Crikey, who's making all that racket?"

He yanked open the window.

The whizzing suddenly stopped. Unravelling himself from behind the fence was Grayson, holding a line trimmer. They shared a few dry blinks, and Carl leaned over the sill. "What's your sign?"

Grayson pulled down his earmuffs. "Excuse me?"

"Are you the Scorpio supposed to stir up stuff?"

Judgy eyebrows lifted.

"You so are. Annoying." Carl shut the window, and ten seconds later opened it again. He tossed out some flannel. "Stop flaunting your chiselled abs."

About ten minutes later, Grayson appeared at Carl's front door with his flannel shirt buttoned to the chest. "May I come in?"

Carl was staring at his shirt, the way it sat perfectly over that torso. It'd been better when he was flaunting! That way, at least, Carl's favourite flannel would still look best on Carl.

He stopped his fingers from repeating the fast furious antics they'd tried on Jason's suit jacket.

"May I?"

Carl snapped his head up and narrowed his eyes. "What?"

"You and I need to talk."

There was a depth to Grayson's gaze that suggested this was something serious. Carl's stomach twisted as he shuffled back and let him inside.

They moved into the kitchen, where Carl quickly skirted to the opposite side of the kitchen island. His smoothie was one step away from completion, and Carl smile-nodded to Grayson while fruit swirled together with a stop-and-start noise that rivalled the one Grayson had been making outside.

"You asked if I was here to stir up stuff . . ." Grayson's words came in and out of focus between whizzes. "Met a few times . . . That first time . . . rescue . . ." A touch to his forearm. Startled, Carl dropped his finger from the blender button and swung his head to Grayson who was . . . looking at him. Somewhat beseechingly. "Remember?"

Carl blinked. First time meeting. The bike rescue. Of course he remembered. "Of course I remember."

Grayson nodded, and patted his arm. Carl jerkily pressed the blender button again, like it might ward off the unasked-for sparks.

Then jabbed the accelerated blending button.

"Trouble . . . Careful . . . Cliff."

Carl stopped blending. What? No, he must've said *shift*. He was everywhere all the time. Talking shifts and how they kept meeting made more sense. Carl nodded. "You certainly turn up when I least expect it."

"Just as well!" Grayson removed his hand and pulled a clean glass from the cabinet like he was right at home.

"Huh?"

Grayson poured the smoothie out for him. "We seemed to have gotten off on the wrong foot. Maybe you don't want to hear this from me, and I don't mean to offend you. I just want you to know you don't have to hide it. You have someone to talk to."

"Talk?"

Grayson passed him the glass, his voice quiet, full of patience. "It's better than drinking and doing something you regret."

Carl stilled, hand clammy on the cool glass. What did he *do* last night? What prompted this visit? This serious way of talking? Those dark imploring eyes. "I . . . I should really not drink anymore."

"Along with that . . . perhaps open up? Be honest?"

About the double identity thing? Had he admitted it last night? Given himself away for real?

Grayson waited, eyes less judgy than usual which . . . didn't quite make sense. He was too earnest right now; it was making Carl's breath thicken and come out uneven. Grayson must have pieced the clues together and figured it out.

Carl set his smoothie aside; his turn to grab Grayson's forearm, but his wasn't a soft pat. His was a pleading *squeeze*. "Please don't tell anyone?"

Grayson rested a warm hand atop his and drummed his fingers over Carl's goose-bumping skin. Was that meant to be calming?

How could he be calm?

There were goosebumps. And Grayson *knew*. He did. He had to. "How'd you know?"

Grayson took back his hand with a skate of a nail across Carl's knuckles. "It was pretty obvious. And good thing I caught you."

Being caught impersonating his brother was a good thing? "Why?"

"Why?" Grayson's voice rose. "It's not only about you. Others will be hurt."

Carl bowed his head. If others found out he wasn't Jason, of course they'd feel stink. But . . . but they were *already* feeling stink, and . . . Jason would be back soon. He'd carry on with the charade. Pretend it was him at the Street Greet, at Leo's school assembly. That way . . . "I may not hurt anyone."

"That's how you might feel. But"—Grayson touched Carl's chin, lifting it until they were eye to eye—"I promise, someone cares. Someone's heart will break."

They were quiet for a few unsteady, fidgety beats.

Grayson cleared his throat. "Should I not have mentioned it?"

"I mean, since it's obvious, I get why you would. I'll consider what you said. In the meantime, don't tell anyone?"

"I won't gossip. But I have a request."

"What's that?"

"When you have these urges to . . . I mean, since I know . . . please find me first? I'll help you."

"You'll . . . help?"

"Always. I'll make sure no one gets hurt."

"How?"

"I have ears and know how to use them."

Was that some kind of musical reference? Could he help Carl sound like an authentic musician?

Grayson asked, "What's that frown for?"

"I'm surprised you'd want to help with this."

"There are others who would also help. I can give you a few numbers—"

"No! No, no. It's enough that you know."

Grayson grimaced, and nodded.

And Carl couldn't stop staring at him. The rush of dark hair, the darker eyes. The sharp line of his nose, the firm lips. The flannel—Carl's flannel—on that impeccable body. And . . . and the *lean*. The way Grayson angled himself towards Carl, all sincerity, like he was solely concentrated on this moment with him. The air between them felt positively weighted.

All that intensity on the heels of kindness . . . Carl fanned himself. "Starting to see why you have groupies."

Grayson smiled, and Carl quickly raised a halting hand. "I meant I understand how other people might fall for all . . ." Carl swept a hand in Grayson's general direction "that. Not that *I'm* one of them."

Grayson's sweet smile turned into a grin. "If you say so."

Carl shook his head, narrowing his eyes, but he pulled out another glass and poured Grayson some smoothie too. "Actually, I feel better unloading the truth. Having someone who'll have my back."

"That's the point."

Carl slid the glass over the counter. "Drink up, Scorpio." Three sips in, Carl murmured, "Do you think I should avoid people?"

"No, I think that'd make things worse."

"You think I have to tell them?"

"That's up to you. It's an extremely personal matter."

"Yeah . . . Do you *really* think they'd be hurt if—"

"Yes."

Ah, shit. "You have to help me then. So they won't get hurt."

"So you won't get hurt, either."

So Carl wouldn't get hurt either. Wow. It was like Grayson knew how much pretending to be his accomplished twin brother affected him. He nodded quietly and observed Grayson while he finished his smoothie. Something about the way he took this seriously . . . The sheen to his gaze. Like a shield. Like protectiveness.

He cared for his community, the people in it. Old acquaintances and new.

"I've got another shift at the pub soon. Thanks for the smoothie. Let me know if you need any help."

Did this mean Grayson would help him come up with a

plan for the school assembly? Carl nodded and dazedly escorted him to the front door. He gazed after Grayson jostling past leggy lavender, and then snapped out of it. Not a groupie. *Never a groupie*. "Hey. Don't get too fond of my flannel."

CARL TOOK TOTO—AND A BIKE LOCK—AND RACED AROUND the bays for some fresh air. He stopped for a swim and had almost finished a circuit of the city when he got swarmed by pre-teens in their uniforms again. This time he sought Leo out and scared off a couple of goofing guys who thought giving wedgies was "just having fun."

"Thanks, Jason!"

Carl swallowed a sigh. "Let's go, kiddo."

"Mum works late today so I'm going to Under the Raindough. What's that sound?"

That sound was Carl's phone vibrating against his keys. He fished it out of his pocket and answered the Unknown Caller. "Hello?"

"Oh, Jason dear. It is you."

Um . . . who was *this*?

Luckily, he didn't have to ask. She continued, "It's Linda. We met at the Street Greet."

"Linda, of course! The pretty smile."

"Flatterer. My son arrives tomorrow, and my granddaughter loves to play the piano. You so generously offered to tune it for me. I was hoping you might come by tomorrow morning?"

Carl froze mid-step; Leo lurched to a puzzled stop beside him and looked at him with big eyes. "I'd *love* to help, Linda, bu—"

"Thank you, deary. See you at number three around ten."

Carl blinked at the phone screen after the call cut out. He

groaned and tapped the end of the phone against his forehead. How would he get through this one? Confess and let a nice old woman down? Or figure out a way to get the piano tuned?

Surely keeping the elders happy was the overall better thing to do?

"What's the matter?" Leo asked.

"Sometimes I am really stupid."

"That's okay!"

"It is?"

Leo nodded with big, earnest eyes. "You don't have to be smart. All that matters is you're happy and you're a good person!"

A load slid off Carl's shoulders at these innocently uttered words. He fondly rubbed the top of Leo's head. "Aren't you the little philosopher?"

"That's what my mum says."

"Sage words."

"Hey, that's funny."

"I was trying."

They walked against a heaving wind to the bakery, where Carl spotted Sage through the windows, sitting at a table plugging things into a calculator, surrounded by paper. Leo knocked on the locked door, yell-laughing "Mum!" and she bubbled into a smile and rushed to greet her son. Paper flew off the table in the gust that came through the door and Sage momentarily winced before crushing Leo into a hug, pecking kisses on top of his head.

Carl slunk away, but the image formed a sweet, achy knot in his chest. His cousin-slash-real-mum must've been as young as Sage was when she became a mother. Sage had chosen to be Leo's mum despite how young she was. Cora claimed only to be Carl's cousin. They were close, they talked every other day, laughed over their horoscopes, hugged and even had a special handshake. But Carl couldn't shake the feeling he was missing something. Something like pecks on the top of his head. Something like yelling *"Mum!"* with a huge smile.

Carl traipsed past the pub, paused, and backtracked. Grayson was working the bar, in Carl's flannel, surrounded by groupies, and . . . what the heck. Carl joined them. He squeezed to the front and Grayson's gaze snagged on him immediately. "You okay?" he mouthed.

The man's intuition! Spot on. "Came for help," he mouthed back.

Instantly, Grayson shrugged out of his apron and yelled for someone to take over. He grabbed a jacket from a hook on the wall and nodded for Carl to follow him outside.

Not far from the pub was a public bench with planter boxes either side; Grayson snagged Carl's sleeve and towed him to it. When they were seated, slightly angled, knees bumping, Grayson draped his jacket around Carl's shoulders, which was weirdly chivalrous—and Carl didn't dislike it—and looked at him, waiting.

Carl felt something slightly bulky bulging from the inner pocket of the jacket around him. He instinctively plucked at the soft wadded material. "I'm, ah, coming to you for help."

"I'm here. I can listen."

"Oh, I won't be trying to perform anything."

Grayson's brow crunched.

Carl continued plucking—at the soft material stuffed into the pocket, and at the conversation. "I need your help on deciding if and how I should help Linda tune her piano? She kind of expects me there at ten tomorrow."

A blink. "What?"

Carl blinked back. "You said to come to you for help?"

"Help when you're having sad thoughts. Not help with—what?"

Sad . . . *What?* Thoughts? Carl plucked the soft material free and it spilled onto his lap.

A scarf.

A *familiar* scarf. One he'd once tried to make out in the dark. He'd thought the print had been fish, or birds, but it turned out the soft silvery fabric was patterned with hundreds of little silver mice.

Carl lifted it and stared. Understanding hit him with a giant jolt through his middle, making him jump on the cold seat. His gaze snapped from the scarf to Grayson, who was frowning beyond it. His rescuer from the cliff, after he'd had too many beers. The rescuer who had heaved Carl to safety after he'd slipped. Who'd told him off for drink-hiking. Whose cold fingers had carefully checked his injured ankle. Whose broad back had carried him down the hill.

Good thing I caught you, Grayson had said this morning.

Not caught lying. *Literally* caught.

That whole conversation . . . Grayson had seemed so serious.

Carl shook his head.

No wonder. He wanted to know Carl had someone to talk to, someone who would help him if . . . Grayson had looked at him more intensely since the bike-stealing incident. To Grayson, that wasn't the first time they'd met. He would've been wondering if and when that night would be acknowledged. To him, Carl was a bit of trouble indeed.

"You're the guy with the big heart."

Grayson frowned. "You didn't recognise me?"

"You had this scarf over half your face! It was dark. I was drunk."

Grayson took the scarf, expression crunched as he tried to understand something.

"This is a huge misunderstanding," Carl said. "That night, I never intended to . . . I was opening up my arms for a new start, I . . . I'm sorry I made you worry. And, of course, I thank you for offering your help."

Grayson looked up from the scarf. "If you didn't recognise me from the cliff . . . what conversation did we have this morning?"

Well, now.

Did that mean Grayson *hadn't* clued on yet?

If not, perhaps best he didn't? Carl flattened the collar of Grayson's shirt. "You know, flannel looks good on you. You should keep it."

"Jason," Grayson said in a warning tone.

Carl gulped and darted his gaze to the buildings across the street, the lights popping on up the hill . . . Grayson kept staring, slightly judgy eyes *seriously* judgy now. Carl couldn't take it. Besides, even if Grayson didn't know about this double identity thing he was dabbling in right now, he surely wasn't far off figuring it out.

Carl leapt to his feet, jacket pooling to the bench, and bolted at a run up the hill after blurting, "I'm not Jason Lyall."

No one can love who has not a heart.

L. Frank Baum

The Wonderful Wizard of Oz

Chapter Six

Carl didn't sleep much and when he did, he was plagued by dreams of Grayson in grey, staring at him with intense dark eyes. Carl kept running from him, but every corner he turned, *wham*, he toppled into the man again. Good thing the guy was attractive or it would've been frightening for sure. As it was, smacking into him was wildly pleasant for a few moments before that gaze once more sent him fleeing.

He woke screaming for Scorpio to stop stirring stuff up! And wagged an extra warning at his tented bedsheet. "This guy is something else."

He made Carl feel like he was on a boat. In choppy seas. Which was fair. Carl had mostly admitted the truth before he bolted last night, and he didn't know what to expect from Grayson going forward. That in itself was enough to make his stomach churn.

But there was something else . . . exhilarating and terrifying. Throwing him off balance. Overboard!

Grayson was his cliff-top hero. The guy with the big heart.

There was more to Grayson than vanity and a tinny

façade. He was kind. Constantly helping others. How earnestly he had talked with Carl yesterday . . .

And that penetrating gaze. Carl had thought it judgy, but . . . Grayson searched for the *real* in people. No wonder he needed to keep looking at him.

"Enough. Think of other things."

Like how he'd tune Linda's piano.

He groaned, rolled out of bed, and decided it was early enough. He'd take Toto for a ride.

The wind was roaring outside, and biking became near impossible around some bends, but it was pretty good procrastination. Soon enough, though, the time had come, and he was knocking apprehensively on Linda's door.

She ushered him inside, taking Toto and sitting it with his jacket beside a giant fish tank. "Piano's this way. Come, come."

With a plastered smile and a bag full of tuning instruments he'd found in Jason's closet, Carl followed Linda to a lacy living room and sank onto the piano seat with a rampant pulse.

Linda patted his head and her eyes glazed. "You're a good man, and you're on the right path. Keep walking, the grass will only get greener. Then you'll find your happiness. You'll see."

Wee bit dotty, but a dear. Carl wiped his clammy palms over Jason's ridiculously tight jeans and nodded. "Um, could I get a cup of tea?"

Linda swept out of the room saying she'd return with a hot Earl Grey shortly, and Carl whipped out his phone to the tab he'd opened on how to tune a piano. Everything he'd looked up said tuning was a challenging job that should be done by a skilled professional. Clearly Jason had such skills, but Carl . . . well, faking it could be an expensive ordeal.

He had a plan for this.

He opened the piano lid—check. He held the electronic chromatic tuner device thingy—check. He pressed a few keys while maintaining a sombre expression—check. And when

Linda re-entered the room—check—he sucked in sharply, looked at her with a grimace, and said, "I'm sorry, Linda. My equipment is malfunctioning. Looks like we'll have to call in another professional."

Linda set his tea on a doily on the coffee table. "Oh dear. Will that be very expensive?"

Probably. Who knew? Of course, Jason would. And he'd probably have colleagues he knew who might do it for a deal. He certainly wouldn't leave Linda hanging like this. "Let me call in a favour."

He plugged in a number for a piano technician he'd found that morning, and hit call. He'd simply hire someone, pay out of his own pocket, and pretend—

No one was picking up!

Linda was looking at him like he was her saviour!

What was plan B?

The ringing had long ended, but he held the phone to his ear, smiling and nodding and murmuring, "Won't be long, Linda. We'll sort this out. Absolutely in time for your granddaughter."

Inside, he was one *very long* groan. Stupid, stupid, stupid—

The doorbell chimed through the bones of the house, and Linda blessedly left the living room to answer. Carl sagged to the piano stool. Maybe he should call his brother. Tell him he was getting in all kinds of trouble, and could he somehow actually call in a favour?

He had his thumb hovering over the call button when Linda returned. Carl glanced over with an automatic wave, then whipped his head back and stared.

Grayson slung a bag off his shoulder and crossed over to him. "You promised you'd help me perfect the art of tuning, remember?" He raised both his eyebrows with a pointed 'play along'.

"Ah, so I did," Carl said slowly. "Unfortunately, my thingy is malfunctioning."

Grayson patted his bag. "Mine works."

Yours? You tune pianos as well as . . . everything else?

Carl was a series of rapid blinks.

"Shall we start?" Grayson asked. "May I take the lead and you give me tips where you see need for improvement?"

More blinking.

Grayson set Carl's bag aside and perched next to him on the piano stool, the lengths of their arms mashed together. Under his tongue, for Carl's ears only, he murmured, "You're drooling."

Carl slapped a hand over his mouth and then scowled. He was not.

Grayson smirked.

There was that mischievous, vain side of Grayson again—the side that loved the idea Carl was his newest groupie. Carl dug an elbow into his side and spoke in Grayson's ear. "Tune this and I might drool for real." He turned his head to Linda and grinned. "It's important no one else is around while we do this as any background noises can affect the quality of tuning."

Linda breezed out of the living room with a dreamy smile, telling them to take their time.

Grayson pressed the C key and side-eyed Carl. "You bullshit convincingly."

"Get this done, and then you can chastise me all you want."

Grayson busied himself with tuning the piano. He removed cabinet doors; dusted strings; checked for damaged or muted strings, and gently tuned the flat keys. By the end of it, the piano sounded crisp, and Carl couldn't lie. He was impressed. "I'm impressed." He eyed those dextrous, handy fingers, and briefly remembered their gentleness guiding him out of a crouch. "How do you know how to do this? Don't say *you're* an accomplished pianist."

Grayson shook his head. "Sam played the piano. That's why I learned the skill."

"Sam?"

Grayson stared down at the ivory keys. "My ex."

There was heartbreak here. Carl could hear it—no, feel it. A familiar heavy throb in the air around them. He found himself nodding.

And leaning in. "Sam—Samuel? Or Sam—Samantha?"

Grayson glanced at him out the corner of his eye, and shook his head. He wrapped an arm around Carl's neck and patted his shoulder. "Just Sam."

The playfully patronising pat had Carl grumbling and tossing off Grayson's hand. "That wasn't fishing for useful information."

"No-no, of course not."

"I mean it. It was *curiosity*."

"Sure."

God, this man was infuriating! Also, super amazingly helpful in today's predicament. But really annoying! "I come from a tiny town. Being nosy is a requirement. It's in my blood to pry into people's business."

Grayson looked at him, head cocked, a small smirk at his lips. "That begins to explain things. This town, is it in Oz?"

The conversation was bound to turn in this direction. From the moment Grayson entered Linda's living room, Carl knew an explanation was on the horizon. He flattened his lips and took a few calming breaths, then swivelled on the stool, knocking their knees. "Tassie. I run a convenience store there. I'm actually Carl Birch; Jason Lyall is my twin. We've . . . swapped lives. Temporarily."

"Sounds like the plot of an old movie."

"That might've been where I got the ingenious idea."

"Ingenious?" Grayson looked sceptical.

Carl sort of understood since, well, look at the trouble he'd got himself into. *However*, this was still better—infinitely better—than helping his ex prepare to marry another bloke. "Anyway, the point is I'm not an accomplished pianist, and I'm grateful for your help today. You think you can keep this identity swap thing to yourself? I'm only here another week or two, and when the real Jason returns, he'll carry on the charade. No one will get hurt, you'll see."

A long sigh. "So *that*'s the conversation we supposedly had yesterday."

Carl smiled sheepishly, and then prodded Grayson's arm. "I have a question." Grayson motioned for him to go ahead, and Carl scooched closer, breathing in a whiff of oaky aftershave. "I drank a bit the other night. What did I do to trigger that conversation, exactly?"

"You sat alone in the corner of the pub moaning over your phone."

Carl . . . vaguely recalled scrolling through a Remember This Day photo collection of him and Pete.

"Then you told the couple at the neighbouring table to make sure they weren't mistaking their relationship. That it might just be friendship."

Carl winced. There was a partial memory of a young couple . . .

"You said they should figure it out right away and not be blindsided years later when the other person meets the 'true love of their life'."

Carl smacked a hand to his forehead. The words were true, but the fact he'd *said* them . . .

"And then—"

"There's more?"

Grayson smirked. "Something about getting accomplished. Being desirable and having journalistic integrity. It got a bit bizarre at that point—the beauty of boulevards and three-lane highways? And then—"

"Oh God."

"—you said you'd 'walk it off'."

"I do remember walking."

"Mm. I was afraid you might head up the hills again, so I followed."

"Ah. Right." Carl paused and narrowed his eyes suspiciously. "Did you weed-wack next door *on purpose*?"

"When I helped you home, I noticed the neighbour's yard was due a trim."

"Sure."

Grayson winked, and Carl was hit with a thought that had him grabbing Grayson by his grey collar and gaping at his handsome face, suddenly only an inch away. "*You helped me home*?"

"You couldn't find your keys." Grayson pried Carl's fingers off him. "They were in your pocket."

"You reached into my pocket?"

"You really wanted me to."

"Outrageous."

"My thoughts exactly. I used a gardening fork."

"I . . . I . . . honestly don't know what to say to that."

"You're welcome."

Carl laughed and buried his face in his hands. When he looked at Grayson again, he'd reined in most of his fickle feelings and spoke seriously. "Thank you. For helping me home. For having that conversation with me. For today, too." He nodded. "Under it all, you're a big heart."

Grayson frowned, and all traces of vanity vanished. There was something raw and tender in the way he stared at the piano keys and shook his head.

"Why do you keep dismissing it when I say that?" He'd done the same thing coming down the hill that first night, too.

A sigh and tired pause followed, and Carl's instinctive urge was to pat his shoulder. The instant his hand touched down, Grayson stiffened and rolled the slouch out of his shoulders with a hollow laugh. "A big heart would let you get away with these lies." He leapt to his feet and grabbed his bag, flinging a misty gaze Carl's way, masking it with another laugh.

On the one hand, Carl felt there was something deeper at play here. Something to probe beneath the reaction. On the other hand, he had to protect himself. "What do you mean you won't let me get away with it?"

Grayson walked out of the living room. "I plan to extort you."

Carl learned the next morning exactly how he'd be extorted. It wasn't for money.

He sadly tucked his wallet into his back pocket and followed Grayson into Over The Raindough's kitchen.

Grayson shook out a floor-dusted tin-foil-like apron, came behind Carl, and slipped it over his head. "Arms up."

"Can't believe you'd rather have me glaze your cupcakes."

"I would rather." Grayson tied a bow behind Carl's back, murmuring cheekily in his ear. "And there's a whole lot more you'll have to swallow."

"Aren't you a master at doing these jobs yourself?"

"Always better with a helping hand."

"Fine." Carl picked up an icing pouch thingy. "Show me how."

"Don't squeeze so hard."

"I didn't think it'd shoot out so fast."

"Try again. Gently. Until the tip glistens. Now start glazing. *The cupcakes*!"

"Your hand was in the way. Just lick it off."

"You missed the cupcake again."

"I want a taste too."

"Let go. I'll do it. What's that look for? You didn't want to do this to start with."

"I changed my mind. I also really fancy biting into that cupcake."

"Leave my cupcakes alone. Out."

Carl rounded to the other side of the counter and plunked himself on a high stool. "Sure I can't pay you to keep quiet?"

Grayson laughed from deep behind some ovens, making it sound somewhat maniacal. "You're my PA for a week, Carl Birch. I'll make sure you're too busy to pretend to play piano."

"About that . . ."

Grayson emerged from behind kitchenware and resumed glazing his cupcakes with a quick look Carl's way.

"I have to be a professional pianist again tomorrow. Last time, and that's it."

Grayson stopped glazing and stared at him.

"This time it's important," Carl explained. "It's for Leo's school assembly."

"School assembly . . . Are you actually out of your mind? I asked you yesterday to press C and you pressed F."

"I'm not saying the gig is without difficulties—"

"You are not a pianist!"

"Well, sometimes pretending is the best thing to do. It can be healing. That's what I'm doing for Leo."

Grayson wagged the icing pouch in his direction. "Being yourself always wins in the end. I'll prove it to you. Ah! I have another job for you."

Grayson briefly abandoned his cupcakes, came to the counter and pulled out a box of receipts and a laptop. He started it up, did some clicking, and turned it to Carl. "Simple enough. Plug the totals from those receipts into this spreadsheet, in the correct category, to tally up these expenses."

Carl stared at all those swimming numbers and nodded. He did this stuff at home, too. Not in Excel though. All those grids looked a bit daunting, but he'd manage. One by one, Carl collected numbers and used his phone calculator to determine the totals. An hour passed, and the bakery opened for business, and Carl squirrelled away in a corner to finish the box.

An hour after that, with a few receipts to go, Sage arrived, all bright smiles and boundless energy. She played a song from her phone and Grayson whisked her into a dance; they moved and laughed like they did this as a daily tradition. Carl kept peeking over, amused, mesmerised. What comfort with one another; what fun to have at work.

Grayson caught him watching mid-spin and smiled smugly, and Carl ripped his attention back to the computer. *Scorpio will not stir him up.* Any-which-way. Out of sheer stubbornness, if for no other reason!

But of course, there were other reasons.

Pete had broken his heart. He was here to nurse it. Not hand it over to this handsome heartbreaker to do worse damage.

After the song-and-dance ended, Grayson signed out of his morning shift, slipped behind Carl, and peered over his shoulder. "Thank you for—what are you doing?"

Carl glanced over his shoulder at Grayson's puzzled frown focused on his Excel sheet.

"Tallying the numbers."

"You didn't need to do your own calculations. This tab is set up to run those for you. You only need to pop the numbers into this column."

Heat whipped Carl's cheeks and he shut the laptop, glad Grayson couldn't see his face.

"Nothing to worry about. I'll fix it later. Let's move on." Grayson called to Sage, "I'm borrowing the laptop."

"Sure! What happened to yours?"

Grayson patted Carl's shoulder. "Need a second one today."

Carrying two laptops, Carl followed Grayson quietly to his next gig—typing for Mr Wilson, a former Air Force pilot who'd recorded his daring adventures by hand and now wanted them typed into a document so he could self-publish his life story. They followed him through his old home to the back garden, where a standalone unit held a bed, desk, corner kitchen, and a dozen boxes of journals.

"How long do you think it'll take?" Mr Wilson asked.

Grayson took the laptops and set them on a long desk. "I'm halfway through. With Jason's help, we might even make it by the end of the month."

"Good, good. I'd like to see it released before I kick the bucket." Mr Wilson pointed a shaky hand at the kitchenette in the corner. "Tea and coffee, and in that cupboard there's a bunch of vitamins. Help yourselves."

"Thanks," Grayson said, pointing for Carl to bring one of the boxes from the bed to the desk. "We will."

Carl heaved the box as Mr Wilson inched his walker out the door. "Remember, the door's bung. Don't shut it all the way. Call the landline if you get locked in, I can't hear you yelling from here."

"I know the drill."

Mr Wilson raised a hand in a wave and stop-and-started his way back to the main house.

Carl dropped the box on the desk beside Grayson. "Seriously, how many jobs do you have?"

Grayson pulled out his phone, tapped the screen, and passed it over. Carl stared at the colour-coded timetable filling up fifteen-plus hours of every day. "When do you sleep?"

"I finish at seven and start at four thirty. That's plenty of time to have dinner, clean up, and go to bed."

His monthly schedule looked insane. It ran weekends, too.

Only this coming Saturday was free from things, but one free day hardly seemed enough. "How many jobs do you have?"

Grayson waved it off and slid his phone back into his pocket. "Let's get started. Mr Wilson's handwriting is a bit special, but I'll clue you in." He touched his throat with a wince. "First, tea."

Carl's tea went cold before he could even think to drink it. Mr Wilson's handwriting was not *special*, it was atrocious. While Grayson rat-a-tap-tapped on his keyboard, gaze flying over lines of journal with apparent ease and words flying onto the laptop screen with incredible accuracy, Carl squinted at the yellowed pages, searched for the letters, and prodded them two-fingered. Grayson had done ten pages by the time Carl finished one.

"How's it going?" Grayson asked, taking a break to make himself another tea. "Is it too cold in here?"

Cold? Carl was *sweating*. Hyper-aware of his lack of touch-typing skills, and conscious of all the red-squiggled lines where he'd spelled things incorrectly. "It's going fine," Carl lied. Enough to feel incompetent. He didn't need to voice it.

"Honey, honey, honey."

Carl whipped around in his chair, startled. For a moment there, he thought Grayson was throwing out the endearment to commiserate with him. But Grayson was searching the cupboards.

Another hot tea landed beside him, and Carl was fairly sure this one would go cold too.

"Another couple of hours here, then we'll stop for lunch and head to the library."

"What do we do there?"

There, they offered help to the local community. Editing CVs. Giving feedback on cover letters. Helping build websites.

None of which Carl had any clue how to do himself. Even with the templates Grayson gave him as a guide, Carl was way out of his depth. He smiled and nodded his way through his line anyway, and sent most of the people who approached him over to Grayson.

By the time they'd wrapped up, Carl wanted to sink into the ground and never rear his head again. The day couldn't get worse.

And then his twin rang.

Carl smuggled the ringing phone outside, jostled up as much humour as he could pretend and answered, laughing. "Uh-oh. What have I done now?"

Jason answered far too quickly. "Nothing." Then he paused. "I mean, other than flashing your mum."

Carl . . . honestly had no words to respond to that.

Jason cleared his throat and continued, "The reason I'm ringing is . . ." There was a pause before the rest came out in a rush. "Cora needs to know you love her. That you know she had twins and adopted us out, and you've found your brother, and you still respect her. Hold her dear in your heart."

The idea was suffocating. Telling his real mum that he knew . . . What would that mean for their relationship? How might it change their dynamics? Make things awkward?

Make things better?

"I can't—"

"Sooner or later she'll find out. Don't let her turn down living with a good man and his daughters because of an uncomfortable conversation."

Cora had been seeing her partner for a while now; they seemed good together. It was strange, though, watching her take part in other children's lives. Over the past year, without seeing it herself perhaps, she'd taken on the role of step-mum, and watching her with those girls . . . hurt.

She gave them hugs, took them for outings, ate dinners around a family table that Carl was never at.

Carl shut his eyes and swallowed hard. Why couldn't she

have looked after them? Been like Sage, embracing motherhood despite her young age. His voice stuck in his throat. Scratched its way out. "I . . . Don't say anything. Not yet. I will tell her. After the wedding. I just need a little longer. Keep up the act, please? It'll be easier once Pete's married."

There Carl went again. Excuses. A verbal running away.

It would be just as difficult then as it would now. Carl was simply spineless.

The library doors rolled open behind him and Carl hurriedly stuffed his phone away.

Grayson emerged, clearing his throat and rubbing it. "Packed up for you. We're done here."

Carl had to gobble back his relieved sigh when Grayson added, "Just one more appointment."

More? Carl was utterly depleted. Heavily, he followed Grayson to where they'd locked their bikes. "What will you have me do next?"

"Something fun."

"Fun?"

"You sound suspicious." Grayson's phone buzzed and, still smiling, he answered. "Hello! How can I—really? Right. I suppose I can swing by now. Mm. Be there soon." He hung up and looked over at Carl while tapping the phone against his chin. He nodded to himself, like he'd thought of a good idea.

"What is it?" Carl asked, swinging Toto onto his head.

"That fun thing. You'll have to stand in for me until I get there."

Carl smiled wanly. "Where should I head, boss?"

It is my great sorrow, and makes my life very unhappy. But whenever there is danger, my heart begins to beat fast.

L. Frank Baum

The Wonderful Wizard of Oz

Chapter Seven

This was as far from fun as it could get. Grayson clearly did not get that Carl, the true Capricorn Carl was, was easily disillusioned. Confidence plummeted if he couldn't meet his challenges, and Carl had struggled with every challenge so far today.

Quiz night at a sports bar . . .

This was almost cause to bolt.

The only thing that propelled him inside was imagining Sage and Leo's disappointment upon finding out he was not famous pianist Jason Lyall. Sage would get laughed at, and Leo made fun of by bullies at school. No, he had to go in and play along, just as he would give that speech in assembly tomorrow.

Carl rocked up to the bunch of dudes in green that Grayson had said would be waiting for him, and got a few gruff hellos in response. "You any good at history? We're in the finals tonight. One win away from an all-inclusive weekend holiday. Damn, it's a bad night for Grayson to be late."

A bell rang through the hoppy-smelling pub and one of the dudes shoved out a bar stool for him to sit. Carl leaned on the sticky table and tried to recall what he learned in school history as questions came flying through a microphone. One of the green team answered all music related Qs. Another, sports. Another, geography. Another, literature. Then came history, and it. Did. Not. Go. Well.

Every question was multiple choice, and each and every one he guessed. Wrong.

The yellow table behind them cheered and trumpeted upon scoring the highest points, and his fellow Green Gruffs muttered under their breaths.

Carl ran a hand through his hair with an apologetic grimace.

"He sends *this* guy in his place?" someone muttered.

"Shh, he's right there."

"We were *that close* to winning. He only needed to get two right. *Two*."

Carl climbed off his stool with all the dignity he could muster and rang out a self-deprecating laugh. "History's not my area."

"There's a fun round in twenty minutes. Trivia—"

A whispered scoff carried down the line of guys to his ears. "Seriously, you're asking him to *stay*?"

Carl's neck and ears were on fire. He forced a smile and waved the offer of another round away. The space across the pub floor to the exit couldn't have been more than two dozen steps, but they took forever to walk. Each sticky squelch had more eyes glancing his way. *Who's the guy leaving already? Think he's the one that tanked the Greens. Bless him.*

One of the Green Gruffs chased after him and caught up as Carl sucked in the crisp breeze outside. "Sorry about those guys. They don't wear disappointment well."

Carl didn't think his stomach could drop further. Disappointment. Wow, yeah, he elicited that. He shrugged and ducked into the convenience store next door.

"I'll tell them they should keep their thoughts to themselves."

Carl found himself dithering in the shop without any clear goal, but he pretended to be in the market for something he hadn't found yet, and—magazines. He zipped to them and picked up one of his faves, flipping through.

"Are you sure you don't want to do another round?"

Even *if* they kept their thoughts to themselves, it didn't mean they wouldn't think them—

Green Gruff Number Two entered the convenience store, flagging for his mate. "There you are. Why'd you—" He caught sight of Carl and his expression shifted to disapproval. He grabbed his friend by the arm. "Come on. Leave him to his . . . zodiacs. Explains it all."

The Green Gruffs left the store, one towing, the other being towed, and as soon as they were out of sight, Carl's hands started to shake. The horoscopes before him became a blur of colour; he snapped the magazine shut and stuffed it back on the shelf.

He ran after the Green Gruffs and shouted as they headed back into the pub, "Music. I'd have aced the musical questions. I'm a pianist!"

He dropped his head and turned to Grayson who was paused beside his ute, scarf up over his nose, a dark, slightly judgy gaze on Carl.

Carl stormed past him and that truth-seeking penetration. "I don't want to hear it."

This whole day had shown him it was better to be Jason Lyall. Being Carl . . . was embarrassing.

He struggled with the lock around his bike and shook it before trying again. Then he shoved Toto on his head and wrangled his freed bike down the footpath.

Grayson coughed and called his name, once, twice.

Three times Carl ignored him—

A hand landed on his shoulder and turned him around until Carl was looking into perplexed and worried eyes. "What happened?"

From inside Grayson's jacket—*Jason's* (was he *trying* to tease him?)—light flickered and a phone buzzed. Like a mechanical heart going haywire. A little like how his own silly one was behaving.

"It's probably your mates wondering why on earth you sent *me* to step in. Answer, they'll fill you in."

Grayson didn't answer. He ignored the buzzing lights bursting from his chest and held Carl's shoulder tighter. "What are you talking about?"

Carl shrugged Grayson's hand off him and returned to shoving his bike.

"Please don't leave like this. Where are you going?"

"Home. Have fun with trivia."

"Aren't you my PA for the week? Come join—"

Carl spun around, bike falling against a lamppost, helmet tumbling from his head and catching on the handles. "Are you kidding me? I've hated all the jobs you've given me, but this one was the worst. Did you send me there for a laugh? See how much of a fool I am?"

Grayson backed up a half-step, surprised. "What are you—"

"I couldn't figure out Excel. Can't touch type. Have never written my own CV let alone one for someone else! The whole day I've had to feel inferior. Not everyone is you, talented at a glance." Pulse pounding with frustration, Carl stepped up to Grayson and prodded his chest. "At first, I thought this extortion thing was to mask your own—whatever pain that was at Linda's. Then, I accepted you probably enjoyed being cheeky, making me work for your silence. But now I wonder if I was wrong about you having a big heart. You're just like the rest of them. Trying to make me see myself for the dud I am." Carl grabbed fistfuls of shirt, swallowed the achy knot in his throat, and stared back hard into those dark eyes. "Is it really so bad running a convenience store? Does liking horoscopes make me so undeserving?" He breathed hard. His hands hadn't stopped trembling. "Is this why it feels a little addictive playing Jason? To have people look at me and think 'that's a cool person'. To be accomplished. To be worth—worth . . ."

Carl laughed hollowly. What was he doing? Letting his feelings run away with him wouldn't change anything. And letting them run away in front of someone he barely knew . . . Ridiculous.

He let go of Grayson and stepped back. "Whatever. Go in. Have a blast. I'll stop the melodrama."

Carl turned back to his bike, only to be tugged by the hand and spun around. In a whoosh of movement and woodsy scent, Grayson's arms came around him and hauled him into a hug. Carl startled, and Grayson held on tighter, a puffed sigh rolling along the back of his neck. It took Carl many uneven breaths before he could utter "Grayson?"

"Can we . . . sit somewhere a moment?" Grayson loosened his hold and gestured down the street to a bench surrounded by lawn and tussock that overlooked the harbour.

The bench was cold, and they were both underdressed for a southerly wind, but emotions ran hot, tempering it. Mostly. Grayson dabbed a nervous-looking sheen from his forehead, opened and shut his mouth, and then, at Carl's shiver, unwrapped his silver scarf and draped it around Carl's shoulders. "Wait here a minute."

He rushed off the bench and dashed towards the convenience store, returning a minute later with steaming paper cups of coffee. Carl tucked the soft scarf he'd been staring at into his collar, and took the drink.

The first sip was a creamy treat and Carl decided he'd give Grayson the benefit of the doubt.

Grayson stared into his coffee cup and then lifted his gaze to Carl. "I'm sorry I'm late. I'm sorry I left you alone. I'm sorry I've hurt you."

The apology had Carl's throat thickening. "Why? Why did you want me doing all this?"

"I thought being busy might numb your feelings. But I misunderstood your pain and made it worse. I was wrong."

Numb my feelings. Carl watched Grayson's gaze drop to his coffee again. It took a few beats, but eventually Grayson continued, "I messed up with you today." He dabbed his brow with his sleeve again. "About your twin swap. I won't tell anyone."

"No more extortion?"

"I'm truly an asshat."

Carl chuckled and side-eyed Grayson for a long moment. "You know what? It's hard to admit making mistakes. Harder to apologise. I maybe, sort of respect you right now." Breath fogged the air between them as he leaned in and added, "I'm sorry for lashing out at you, too. Saying you have no heart . . . It was said in frustration. It was mean and untrue."

Grayson smiled, but there was a sad depth in his eye. When he noticed the carefulness of Carl's observation, he tried to laugh it off. "You weren't all wrong. It's broken, this one." Laughter turned into coughing, and Grayson shifted away from him on the bench. There was a wall being thrown up, and a big sign to Change The Subject.

Carl wasn't entirely ready to accept the wall, though. He tried lightening the mood instead, thumping a palm on Grayson's thigh. "If you ever decide to fix it, you've got actual groupies to help."

Grayson hesitated, like he was warring inside how hard to shut this topic down. He swallowed and cast a look at Carl's palm. "Including you it seems."

Carl scoffed and pinched Grayson's thigh before letting go.

Once again, Grayson's laugh turned to coughing, and the violence of it had Carl gazing hard at the man. That sheen on his forehead, the dampness around his short eyelashes, the red mark where Grayson kept touching his throat. Not nervousness and a slight cough. This was . . .

Carl smacked a hand onto Grayson's forehead and yelped. "You're hot."

"You don't give up, do you?" Grayson wheezed.

Carl gently pushed Grayson's head back for that naughty comment. "I might have some respect for you and admire your ability to be everywhere at once and appreciate your overall form, but let's be clear. I'm not into you."

"'Course not."

"You're unbelievable."

"Why, thank you."

Carl rolled his eyes and pulled Grayson up. "You really like people liking you." Carl patted Grayson's chest over the heart. "Next is to like liking them back."

"All those likes make me dizzy. Could you . . . drive us back?"

Carl kept a close eye on Grayson all the way back to his bike. He wheeled it to the ute and heaved it into the bed. When he turned back, it was to find Grayson slouched against the passenger door, dozing off.

"Grayson? Grayson?"

A moan was his only response. Those dark eyes stayed firmly shut, and his head rolled forward. Yikes, he was running a real fever. Carl left him dozing while he dashed to the store for ibuprofen and a bottle of water, then tried to get the man to swallow it. Carl lightly slapped his cheek. "Wake up, you need to take this. Bring the fever down."

Grayson folded in half, buckling to the curb where he curled up like he was set to sleep for the night. Okay, then. So Grayson was the type who turned into a big toddler when he was sick. Carl dropped to his knees, water and two white pills ready. "Open up."

Grayson snuggled into his crooked arm.

"Open up or I'll shove my finger in your mouth."

Still no answer.

Fine, he asked for it—

He slipped the pills over Grayson's tongue and squirted water. Grayson swallowed instinctively and the suction pulled on Carl's finger. Gah. "Not a lollipop, let go—not a carrot either!" Carl wrangled his poor throbbing finger free and glared at his sleepy, sick companion. "I swear I'll never stick anything into your mouth again."

For the keys, though—where were the gardening forks when one needed them?—he had to stick his throbbing finger into the confines of Grayson's pocket. He snagged the metal, pulled the keys free, and wrangled Grayson into the passenger seat. "Hands down the most un-sexiest moment of my life."

Grayson made a sound suspiciously like a scoff, and Carl talked himself out of pinching the sick.

By the time they reached Berhampore, Grayson was snoring. Instead of waking him to get his address, Carl drove home to Jason's and parked in the driveway. He grabbed blankets from inside, let the seat down, and made it as comfortable as possible. Seated beside his patient, Carl jotted notes for his assembly speech. He left briefly to visit the bathroom and yelped when he found Grayson had stumbled his way into the hallway. He was half awake and coughing, leaning against one of Jason's framed certificates. "Bathroom."

Carl showed him the way and left him to it, and a few minutes later Grayson emerged to find the nearest soft surface —the sofa—to collapse onto. "I'll crash here a bit."

He was still there at five in the morning, the blankets Carl had provided kicked off to the floor along with Jason's jacket and a damp undershirt. Carl did him a favour and messaged

Sage that he wouldn't make it to the bakery, told the sleeping man he was welcome, and continued preparing for Leo's assembly.

"Need an excuse not to touch the piano," he murmured.

A gravelly voice murmured back a most brilliant solution.

"Excellent. Are you awake?"

"No."

"Then I won't throw you out. Sleep on." He left Grayson with more painkiller, a pot of ginger tea, and a note, and went to shop for necessary items. A few hours later, carrying a few hundred bribes, he gulped his way into Leo's school.

Leo escorted Carl from the gate, non-stop admiration and gratitude for Jason helping him out. The kid's step contained a bounce that Carl hadn't seen before—and it, along with last night's confirmation, convinced Carl that playing Jason Lyall was the right thing to do.

The hall was abuzz with excited chatter as lots of green-and-yellow uniforms took their seats. And Leo led Carl up the front, to the stage. It held a daunting-looking grand piano; Carl faced it down as he moved to the microphone and greeted the audience.

It was thrilling enough to be speaking to kids, but his heart raced harder when he caught sight of three rows at the back for parents. Perched one-two-three in the first of those rows were his favourite witches. Grand.

He searched for Sage and found her standing in the corner along with a few others that didn't get seats. She smiled brightly and waved, and Carl became even more committed to the act. "Hello everyone here today. I originally intended to start this presentation with a short performance but"—he tugged Jason's jacket sleeve up his arm, revealing a bandage—"I sprained my arm and must avoid any strenuous activity."

There were a few sorry sighs at this, some nods of understanding, and one merciless smirk—

Carl straightened. Why was Grayson here? He should be feeling sorry for himself somewhere soft. Not dressed in all of Carl's flannel that he must have found in Jason's closet. Grayson coughed and lounged against the wall next to Sage, raising his brows for Carl to please, continue. He even motioned a zipper across his mouth, a reminder of his promise not to say a word.

Carl gulped again, and cleared his throat. "My helper Leo will be passing out gummy pianos. On the back of each is a number. At the end of this speech, I'll use my phone to draw a winner. Leo?"

Leo stepped forward and held up a clear plastic violin filled with lollies. Not a piano, but music-themed.

"Sweet treats for all the studying I'm sure you're doing."

He and Leo received a laugh from the teachers and a tremendous cheer from the sweet-starved kids. The sound rushed around him, and . . . this is what he'd meant about Jason being addictive. It felt nice—if also nerve-wrecking.

"There were many things I could have talked to you about today—fascinating musical trivia, accounts of my trips performing abroad, the technical ins and outs of being a professional pianist"—he jerked his gaze away from where it strayed to Grayson's sick-yet-amused expression—"But I decided to talk about something that is important for everyone sitting here today, no matter how young or old you are: Courage and facing adversity.

"My journey to mastering music—and any journey you might undertake—is marked by countless challenges, feelings of doubt, and Sisyphean obstacles. These are things we all have to face with determination, strength, and bravery."

Carl had imagined, upon looking at all of Jason's awards, what fortitude it must have taken to get to where he was, and he hoped he was hitting the spot as he shared these thoughts with the kids. "It's fun to dream of mastering the great works of composers and moving audiences with the magic of music, but the reality—the road to that emerald city—means aching fingers, stumbling over keys, repeating pieces for hours. It also means battling self-doubt, and refusing to let other people's negative comments and unimpressed frowns get to you. Each step is a struggle, but the only way to reach your dream is to push on."

Carl's gaze had once again wandered towards Grayson. This time, though, Grayson wasn't amused. Those dark eyes were back to boring into Carl.

Carl jerked his head towards the kids and continued. Facing fears head-on; the necessity of courage in our lives. "Even if it's uncomfortable, even if it feels like the world is against you. Believe in yourself. Trust in yourself. You may not reach your destination, but your heart will only feel at peace if you've taken all the steps you can."

Carl wrapped up his speech to ear-splitting applause that only grew louder after he drew a winner for the violin-case of sweets.

Teachers and parents flocked to him afterwards, thanking him for coming, and it was all a massive head rush. Seventy percent of him was happy to bathe in the attention. The other thirty percent niggled—and niggled harder when one of the witches asked a technical question about whether learning on a keyboard is easier than an actual piano.

Before the question was fully formed, Carl made eye-contact with Sage, waved, and wrangled his way out of the crowd to where she was patting Leo's head proudly.

"Leo," Carl said, "I've heard at least three kids say you're awesome!"

Leo flushed, and his mum cheered.

"Come round to the bakery for cupcakes anytime," she told Carl, and to Leo, "Enjoy the rest of school, hun, come straight home after."

Leo waved her off and swivelled around, scanning the crowd like Carl. The witches were leaving, waving to their kids—the two bullying boys who'd tried stealing his bike and a girl with red plaits. The principal asked the kids to start stacking chairs, and Leo gripped Carl's sleeve and made him promise to not leave him alone with them.

"I know you just talked about courage, but I don't have any yet."

Carl patted Leo's shoulder. "I'll be your shield."

"You're the bravest *ever*."

Carl thought about how he couldn't talk to his real mum about knowing the truth; thought about how he'd run away from his ex because he couldn't face telling him it hurt too much to be his best man; thought about how he play-acted Jason to avoid feeling like a dead end. He smiled sadly and shook his head. He wondered if this was the reason Grayson had stared at him so hard during his speech. Courage. What a topic to choose.

"Don't look up to me too hard, Leo. I'm all talk."

Leo didn't hear him. He was pointing across the hall to where Grayson coughed into his elbow while being cornered by a half-dozen cooing women.

That seemed about right.

Carl shook his head and steered Leo instead towards the stage, where he'd left the bags that had held his bribes. Leo trailed his fingers over the ivory keys of the grand piano, and the bullies stacking chairs stopped to snicker.

Red plaits stared at the boys. "What's funny?"

The boys said—loud enough for it to reach Leo's ears, as

was probably intended—"Getting that guy to speak is as close to playing the piano as he'll ever get."

"Yeah," the other one said, "Can't afford a piano, let alone a teacher."

Further back, Grayson—who'd freed himself from his groupies—paused overhearing this and started a swift stride towards the boys. He wasn't fast enough for Carl, though. The microphone was right there, and he made sure he was close enough to it when he said, "Hey, Leo, if you like that piano, you should check out mine at home."

Leo's miserable face transformed into a hopeful one, while the bullies returned glum-faced to stacking chairs. "Really?"

Carl silently cheered himself for his quick thinking, and then got slightly carried away with the rush. "Not only can you *see* it—" He spied Grayson shaking his head in warning, like he knew what was coming. But it was all too late—the words were tripping out of his mouth.

"I'll teach you how to play it."

The greatest loss I had known was the loss of my heart.

L. Frank Baum

The Wonderful Wizard of Oz

Chapter Eight

Carl was not eager to hear Grayson's (probably very reasonable) response to his declaration he'd become Leo's piano instructor, so he did what he did best.

He flashed Leo a wave, jumped off the stage, and ran away.

He came home to folded blankets, a washed teapot and cup, and a note to the end of his note that contained Grayson's number and address. Carl stared at the numbers for a rather long time before he plugged them into his phone under 'Berhampore's Heartbreaker'. He stared again at the address. What did this mean? Did he want Carl to visit? Or was this for future reference so if Grayson passed out again, he could take him directly home?

Whatever the reason, seeing it sent a sharp shiver through Carl. It was a sign. He'd felt a little silly running away, especially on the heels of how mature Grayson had behaved the evening before. Addressing things with him face-to-face, apologising, generally *communicating*. And that, while he'd been sick.

Carl really should learn something from that . . .

So, of course, he got himself ready, popped on his jacket, and spent the next few hours taking Toto for a ride.

GRAYSON'S HOUSE WAS NESTLED AT THE END OF A CUL-DE-SAC—a pretty brick home with a chimney that was smoking and a stack of firewood along the fence at one side. Emerald green accented the windows and coloured the door. Carl straightened the button-up flannel he'd decided was safe to wear here, and knocked. Nervously.

Grayson opened the door fitted out in the fluffiest grey dressing gown Carl had ever seen. He took a moment to take it all in, from the hood framing the man's face, to his matching bunny slippers.

"Oh my God, you're adorable."

Grayson rolled his eyes and noticed Carl's comfy shirt, lingering on it.

Carl rolled off a wee shiver and lifted the container of soup he was carrying. "I was taught never to show up empty handed."

"Come inside."

He toed off his shoes and followed the grey fluffball down the hall. "You live in a dead end."

"Dead ends are the best. Quiet; peaceful; cosy."

A funny laugh burst out of Carl unprompted, causing Grayson to glance at him over his shoulder with a questioning brow.

Carl cleared his throat. "You won't get it," he said as they emerged into a stainless steel and wood kitchen, "but that is very nice to hear. Where should I put this?"

Grayson gestured to a corner of the bench against the wall, where five full Tupperware boxes were stacked. Carl glanced at his two-person air-tight container and back again. Of course.

The groupies. They'd noticed Grayson was sickly at the assembly and got right to work.

Wait. What did this make Carl look like?

He groaned and sagged onto a stool, plopping the container before him. "I don't mean it like they mean it."

"They mean to help me feel better. How do you mean it?"

"Well . . . I mean . . . the same, but—"

Grayson nodded smugly.

"—oh whatever. I slaved away all afternoon and I'm hungry. Let's eat together."

Grayson nodded and went to take Carl's soup but Carl pulled it out of reach. He jerked a thumb towards the other containers. "Heat up one of those."

"I thought you slaved away?"

"I burned it and had to pick out all the charcoal."

"You brought it anyway?"

"The empty-handed thing."

"Such a gentleman."

Grayson gave orders to put out placemats, salt and pepper, water glasses, while he microwaved the soup, ladled it into bowls, and watched Carl like he was holding back comments. Sure enough, when they were at the table breathing in steaming nutrition, Grayson cleared away a cough and pointed his spoon. "Did it feel good up on stage?"

Carl lifted his gaze across the square dining table and sighed. "Truthfully, yes. Being Jason, I felt confident."

"You could've given pretty much the same speech as Carl."

"With what to back me up? I haven't done anything remotely courageous in my life."

"I haven't known you very long, but what I've seen says otherwise. You've a strong sense of justice. You've been helping and sticking up for Leo since you met him." Grayson leaned in. "To the point of becoming his piano instructor. I don't know how you'll pull it off, but I understand why you offered."

Carl swallowed. "You weren't going to tell me off for that?"

"Is that why you ran off?"

"You were shaking your head at me."

"Well, I'm not without concerns. But your motivations were sincere."

"I should've stayed. Those words are pleasantly relieving."

"Have you thought about how you'll teach him?"

"I have a plan. I'll get Jason to follow it when he returns."

"Your poor brother will have many new responsibilities to assume."

"I'll find a way to make it up to him." Carl eyed fluffy Grayson spooning more of his chicken soup. The way he blew on the spoon, carefully slid it into his mouth and gulped softly with a satisfied twitch at his mouth . . . "The grass is greener, personified."

A blink. "What?"

"This soup is good, but watching you eat it, it looks tastier. I want your bowl."

Grayson curled a protective arm around his soup bowl, blocking Carl's curious and advancing spoon.

"Could you be any more precious?"

"The others call me *handsome*."

"Have they seen you dressed like a bunny nibbling at soup? I should take a picture."

Grayson wagged his spoon back at Carl. "Don't you dare."

Their spoons collided with a vibrating chink, and then they were sword-fighting and laughing—Grayson between a few coughs—until Grayson retreated and gave in. Carl dunked his spoon into his soup and brought it to his lips. His veins hummed with triumph and Grayson's amused head-shake, the twinkle in his dark eye, had Carl smiling—

"Didn't think you'd be so keen to catch this," Grayson said with an emphasising cough.

". . . You make an excellent point." Carl was about to

lower the spoon when he caught an odd, smokey scent. He glanced at the liquid and shot his head up to Grayson. "That is not the same soup." He snagged Grayson's bowl, dragging it over the table to look, to inhale more deeply. "You heated up *my* soup?"

"I was taught to respect people's effort. Politeness. Turns out"—he grimaced—"I'm really, really polite." Grayson took his bowl back and quietly forced himself to eat more.

"You didn't—*don't*—have to eat it."

"You looked after me last night."

"That was . . . was . . . *social responsibility*! Nothing that requires you to sacrifice your tastebuds."

Grayson took another mouthful, staring stubbornly at Carl in a way that had him . . . hiccupping.

And hiccupping.

In fact—he palmed his chest a few times—he couldn't *stop* hiccupping. He tried gulping water and, at another jump in his chest, spilled it down his front. Wow, he was on form tonight.

Grayson lifted a tissue from his pocket, started to offer it, looked at it, and scrunched it back into his pocket. "Bathroom's that way."

Carl lunged down the hall into the bathroom and stayed hidden behind its closed door. Look at him. He'd done a number on his flannel too. He undid the buttons and wrung out the water soaked into it. He released his held breath and stared at his reflection in the mirror. "Hiccup again and you never have to face your ex or your mother."

The wish was so strong that, of course, no hiccup came.

He sighed. At least the hiccups were over.

He quickly did up his buttons and snuck out of the bathroom, only to see, in the brighter light of the hallway, that'd he'd messed up the sequence. He fiddled about undoing the buttons again and paused at an open doorway. This must be the master bedroom. The light was off, but he made out a large king bed and some side cabinets, and—what *was* that painting above the bed?

Curiosity got the better of him. He snuck into the room on light feet, eyes fixed on the dark frame. It was some sort of—

Carl tripped over the upturned lip of a rug. He stumbled forwards, arms flailing as he tried to catch his balance. He reached out to brace against the bed, only to—like a complete muppet—trip over his own foot and fall face-first onto a soft quilt.

"Seriously?" he groaned onto a wedge of pillow. He rolled over and froze at the sight of the painting looming overhead. Who was this Grayson, really? Why did he have a picture like that? Why did he hang it where he *slept*?!

He stared at the image. A doll-like figure, shrouded in shadows, dancing mechanically—maniacally?—across the canvas like someone pulled at its strings. It was all dark against a darker background—eerily like the endless depth in Grayson's eyes—and like those eyes, it made him shiver.

And shiver again. He wasn't sure what was more horrifying. That creepy painting, or the fact Grayson's footsteps were coming down the hall.

He pushed a hand against the bed in an effort to quickly rise and his wrist gave way, causing him sink onto an elbow. The precise moment at which Grayson stepped into the room and switched on the light.

Carl squinted against the sudden brightness and blinked in Grayson's stock-still, open-mouthed *gape.* It took only a moment to reconstruct the scene from the point of view of those baffled eyes. There Carl was, his shirt undone, revealing a decent slice of chest and stomach, while lounging provocatively on the master bed. He might at any moment curl a finger or tiger-growl at Grayson to come join him.

Grayson plucked up a bottle of pills from the dresser. "Came for these."

Carl was absolutely beside himself. He was hurriedly buttoning his flannel while glaring heavenward and wagging a mental finger that way. "This isn't what it looks like."

"What does it look like?"

"Like a crazy person snuck into your room and prostrated himself half-naked in the vain hope of seducing you?"

"So you are aware."

Carl shoved himself into a sitting position. "What this actually is . . ."

"What actually is it?"

"Me giving *you* serious judgy-eyes. What on earth is this painting above your—"

Carl looked up and stopped.

In the light, the painting was nothing quite so menacing as it'd seemed under shadow. In fact, it wasn't a painting at all, but a large photograph. Of a young boy. Dancing on a stage. And he looked like a younger version of the man staring at him with his eyebrow cocked, awaiting a sufficient explanation.

Carl laughed weakly. "That's you as a kid."

"Ah, so you came in here to look at my childhood photos."

"Is there any way I can come out of this room *not* looking like I'm desperately in love with you?"

"Don't beat yourself up." Grayson moved to the bed before him. "You're allowed to have feelings." He bent down, a whoosh of air against his jaw, to speak in his ear. "And I'm allowed to not respond to them."

Carl jerked back. "Feelings? Even if I had feelings, I'd have lost them after one look at your photo in the dark!"

"What's wrong with my photo?"

"I know you quite fancy yourself, but is it common to put up enlarged pictures of oneself above one's bed?"

"I like this photo."

"Of course you do."

"I'll never get sick of looking at it."

"It's a bit shocking there's no mirror in this room. On the wall. Above the bed . . ."

"My mother won a photography competition with that picture."

His mother . . .

God, why did Carl always say the wrong thing? He stuffed a fist against his mouth to stop any more nonsense escaping, cleared his throat, and took in the photo more carefully. "It's . . . I mean, the form is artistic . . . There's a special vibe to it, yes."

Grayson folded his arms.

"I'm a terrible person." Carl sank off the bed onto his knees before him, almost bashing his head against . . . Grayson quickly shot back a foot. Carl winced. "Forgive me," he said. "I invaded your privacy and then had the audacity to get judgemental. This picture is meaningful. Of course you should have it above your bed. Of course it'd never scare the bejesus out of you."

Grayson reached down and helped him to his feet. "I love this picture—"

Carl nodded hard.

"—but it *is* spooky in the dark."

"Oh, thank God!" Carl whacked him on the fluffy forearm. "You scare yourself sometimes?"

Grayson gave him a warning look not to overdo it, and Carl zipped his mouth shut. "This was taken during a talent show at intermediate school."

"Did you get first prize for freaking people—" Grayson doubled-down on his look and Carl grinned. "You danced."

"Tap. I did it for a few years. Stop smirking."

"Can you still do it?"

Grayson shrugged, which had Carl sidling towards what looked like a closet door. "You've got a pair of silver shoes in here somewhere, don't you?"

Grayson jumped in front of him, barring the way. "I'm sure you had such moments as a kid too."

"Of looking like a creepy puppet dancer? Let me think."

Grayson tapped a sharp knuckle on his forehead and Carl rocked back on his heels, laughing. "Okay, I lost my trunks swimming in a competition once. Are we even?"

"Do you have a photo?"

Carl shook his head.

"We're not even."

Snickering, Carl fished out his phone, set it to selfie mode, took a picture of himself making a face and sent it to Grayson. "There. Laugh at me whenever you want."

Grayson checked the photo and nodded soberly. "Good enough to scare away any prospective partner." A rattling cough dominated the next half minute and Carl grimaced, took Grayson by the elbow and led him to the bathroom.

"Brush your teeth, wash up. You're going to bed."

Carl shut him inside, and while Grayson did his business, prepared a glass of water, some lozenges he found, and optional painkillers. He set this on the bedside, and cheekily checked the closet for those silver tap shoes . . .

He found a pair atop a photo album, and when he lifted the shoes, curious at their weight, a lone photo fluttered to the floor.

It was a picture of Grayson with his arms wrapped around a dimpled man. And the look Grayson gave the man . . . that was a look Carl had seen many times before. Whenever Pete gazed at Nick.

Grayson entered the room, and Carl whirled around with a guilty grin. "Saw your tap shoes, and saw that Sam is a Samuel."

"Don't look so gleeful."

"I knew it."

"You *hoped* it."

"Rubbish." Carl returned the things, closed the closet, and threw back the quilt. "In you hop."

Grayson eyed Carl suspiciously as he followed these instructions. And Carl hung up his dressing gown on a hook behind the door. "By the way, I had an epiphany while you were brushing your teeth."

"An epiphany?"

Carl moved to Grayson and perched beside him on the bed. "We've been through a few ups and downs, you and I. Plus you're the only one who knows my secret. We should be friends."

Grayson scooched away from Carl and those dark eyes were positively obsidian. "What kind of friends?"

"Without benefits!"

Grayson raised a brow.

Carl hurried on, "The kind who hang out for as long as I'm here."

"I don't have huge amounts of free time."

"Let's not get worked up over the details." Carl smiled and reached over for a handshake to seal the deal. "You be kind, and I'll be kind. We'll be kind together."

The handshake thrummed, and Carl still felt it around his fingers the next morning. Like they'd transferred a massive amount of energy—energy that seeped into the rest of him and had him eager to *do* things. He biked around the bays, and, still bouncing on his heels afterwards, headed for Grayson's. He'd seen the man's calendar; today had been curiously void of commitments.

Grayson opened the door, smartly dressed this time, but in the most depressing grey Carl had seen on him yet. The man's downcast expression didn't help things, either.

"This isn't the best ti—" Grayson stopped abruptly when Carl palmed his forehead.

He didn't feel feverish.

"You don't look great, Gray." Carl pushed him back and only let go of his forehead when they were halfway up the hall. "I'll make you a cup of tea."

Grayson opened his mouth to say something and clapped it shut again. He followed Carl into the kitchen and helped him find things in the cupboards.

Lots of honey went into the tea—the man looked in desperate need of sweetening. He wasn't coughing so much this morning, but there were a few sighs that had Carl thinking he might be having a blue day.

Carl understood the feeling. Hadn't that been him a few nights ago? "Drink this, then would you like to get our feet done? Paint our toenails?"

Grayson spluttered his honey tea and looked over the bench at him.

Carl said, "Colours are fun. They can make you smile when you look at them. Like when you're home alone, before bed, in the shower—times you might feel particularly lonely."

"Is this something you do?"

"Mmm. With my—my real mum. Anyway, we foot spa together, splash on the rainbow, and it literally brightens my mood."

"Your real mum?"

Carl waved that off and hurriedly tipped tea into his mouth. His eye caught on a framed photo that had been placed against the wall at the end of the bench, where the groupies' soups had stood yesterday. He set down his mug, picked up the photo of a dark-haired woman with familiar dark eyes, and stared at it. Glossy waves framed a soft, pale face, and her deep, dark, expressive gaze seemed to capture Carl's even through the photo. Lines of laughter were etched around her eyes and mouth. Carl had seen this mischievous smile on Grayson, too. Undoubtably, this was his mother.

. . . he doesn't talk about it, but he's been like that since his mother died and he broke up with his ex.

Carl looked over the photo at Grayson staring at the back of the frame, and he set it down gently. "She's beautiful. You look like her."

Grayson picked up the photo. "She liked getting her toes and fingernails done too."

"Did she have a favourite colour?"

"Magenta."

"Tell me about her."

"What are you trying to do, Carl?" Those dark eyes pierced him, and Carl shoved a hand through his hair.

"We're, uh, friends now. You can talk about stuff with me. Purge. Get it all out. I'm the best option, really—soon I'll be gone, so you won't have to feel embarrassed that someone you see all the time knows. Your secrets will stay safe."

Grayson scrubbed his face and breathed deeply into his hands for a few moments before looking up. "Would this be a two-way street?"

Carl sharing his secrets too?

Hadn't he started already? "That sounds . . . like a good kind of road."

Grayson nodded thoughtfully, stood, and gently towed Carl to the door. "Let me think about it."

The emerald door shut in Carl's face.

CARL FROWNED AND HEADED DOWN THE STREET AND UP SOME stairs to the main road, where very soon he spotted Leo ducking into Over The Raindough. He headed over there himself. Sage was busy with a long line of customers, still smiling, and Carl slouched to the table Leo had nicked for himself.

Almost immediately, Leo asked, "When can we do our first lesson?"

Carl took his time seating himself and clasped his hands together. "Theoretical knowledge of music is foundational. For the first couple of weeks"—as long as Carl was here—"that will be our focus."

"I'm good at theory! Test me, test me. I know *everything*."

"That took an unexpected turn," Carl mumbled.

"Turn. A sideways S shape symbol above the notes. Means to quickly play the note above the main note, the main note, and the one below it, and back to the main note."

Carl wince-smiled. "Seems theory is your forte."

"Forte, loud. Fortissimo, very loud. Mezzo-forte, moderately loud."

Carl nodded. "A natural."

"A squarish-looking symbol. Put before a note restores any altered sharps or flats to their natural pitch."

Carl decided he should stop opening his mouth, propped his elbow on the table, and clamped his lips shut with his fingers, smiling and nodding at Leo instead.

"Does that mean we can start practicing right away?"

"Leo," Sage said, shaking her finger at him as she crossed to their table with cupcakes. "I told you not to put pressure on him. It's kind enough he offered at all."

Leo sank his head and apologised but Carl hurriedly stopped him. "It's okay, it's okay. Totally no problem."

"Then we'll start tomorrow?" Leo asked brightly. "Have heaps of lessons since it's school holidays now?"

Carl's breath caught in his lungs and his brain blanked. No excuses came to him, and two sets of big eyes were looking at him hopefully, waiting.

"Of course!" he blurted. "Yes. Tomorrow morning sound okay?"

"You're the bestest, Jason. The best."

"Not as good as these cupcakes." Carl stuffed one into his mouth before his face filled with fret.

"I'll have Leo bring some more tomorrow. I gotta get back behind the counter. Jason, let's talk later."

She left, and half an hour later, so did Carl. He moped around Berhampore and was about to head home when he glimpsed Grayson turning onto the city-to-sea walkway. Spotting him wasn't unusual—he was used to seeing Grayson at any possible point during the day now—but the massive bouquet he carried was. Carl snuck from tree shadow to tree shadow, following sneakily up the hill, past the outcrop where Carl had tumbled, to a craggy sprawling tree amongst long grass. At this tree, Grayson knelt and laid out his flowers. He bowed his head, and Carl swallowed thickly. Suddenly, the framed photo on the bench and the unusual free space in Grayson's calendar made sense.

Carl stayed a few shadows behind and bowed his head too. He waited in silent respect for a few minutes, before slinking away quietly.

"Stay," Grayson called. "I know you're there."

Carl shrank back to the sap-seeping tree trunk and waited guiltily while Grayson swiped his eyes with his sleeve, squared his shoulders, and approached.

"I'm sorry," Carl said.

"For following me? Or for"—Grayson glanced heavily towards the gnarly tree and the bouquet, and Carl's chest banged about painfully. He hauled Grayson into a hug and held him tight, as tight as Grayson had held him two nights before. Grayson didn't resist. He sagged into the hold, chest heaving rapidly as he struggled against a sob. Carl rubbed circles over his back, and kept rubbing them even when Grayson's warm breaths against Carl's neck had evened.

Grayson withdrew from the hug and pulled himself tight, together, in control—*almost.* His body might seem proud and straight, but eyes were the windows to the soul, and Grayson's were devastated.

"Do you want . . . space?" Carl asked quietly.

Grayson shook his head and his voice cracked. "Sit with me for a bit."

They sank to the base of a tree and stared towards the gnarly one and the bouquet. "This was her favourite spot to bring me to play when I was a kid."

Carl tensed. Was Grayson accepting his offer to purge his secrets? He swallowed a fluttery feeling and murmured, "All the way up here?"

"I had a lot of energy. The hill helped get rid of some of it."

"Clever."

"She was. Back then, we were so close."

Carl faced Grayson's sigh and felt a sympathetic one of his own bubble in his chest.

"Then I grew up. Moved away. Met someone. Mum kept asking me to drive down and visit, and I barely did. Then one day she called asking for help with a wasp nest in her back garden. I didn't really want to make a long trip to do it and offered to pay for her to get someone to come, but she refused. She tried getting rid of it herself and fell from the ladder." Grayson's face crunched towards a sob and his voice thickened. "She died before I could get to the hospital."

Carl wound an arm around Grayson, and Grayson dropped his head on his shoulder for a few struggling breaths. "She asked for help, and I wasn't there."

Carl whispered, "A tragic accident."

"She'd still be alive if I'd come."

Carl's throat hurt, and he shook his head even though Grayson couldn't see it. "It's not your fault."

Was this why Grayson took up every odd job asked of him by the community? As penance for not helping his mum? Hoping his help might save others in future, like he'd saved Carl that night at the cliff?

Was this why Grayson worked most hours of the day? To keep himself busy so he wouldn't feel so guilty?

"You are not to blame."

A gulp. "Sam tried to comfort me after it happened, but I didn't feel I deserved that love. I made the decision to break up and move back here, and my heart hasn't functioned properly since. People keep offering theirs to me, and I'm not immune to the rush of that attention, but I'm allergic to accepting it. So I go on and break their hearts with silly smiles or jokes or tease them for becoming my groupie."

This poor man. How long could he keep torturing himself like this? Carl's hand moved of its own accord and tapped Grayson's chest, over his fractured heart. "Wouldn't your mum be sad seeing you like this?"

Grayson shifted and sat upright. "Wouldn't she be happy seeing me help those who need it? Being there for her friends in the community?"

"If I were a parent, watching my child from above, I'd weep."

"Why?"

"The best thing in life is to love and be loved. And as a parent, I'd want the best for my kids. So if she saw that you couldn't love or be loved . . . wouldn't that make her the most devastated?"

Grayson tipped his head back against the tree trunk and his Adam's apple bobbed. "You think I've been dealing with this wrong?"

"Who am I to say? I ran away from home." Carl stood up,

dusted himself. "Moving on from heartbreak . . . it's a journey." He gazed at Grayson's upturned profile and offered him a hand. "We're on the same road. How about we walk it together for a while?"

Grayson eyed Carl's hand for a few hesitant seconds before he gripped it and let himself be pulled to his feet. Hands locked together, he looked dubiously into Carl's eyes. "What exactly does that involve?"

Carl tugged Grayson close. "Scared I'll kiss you?"

"Yes."

That spurred a gentle snicker from Carl. "If I ever—God forbid—become besotted, you go right ahead and slap me out of it."

"I break hearts, not faces."

"All right, all right. I'll slap myself silly. Come along, we've something important to do."

"What's that?"

"Colouring our toes."

"You people with hearts have something to guide you, and need never do wrong; but I have no heart, and so I must be very careful."

L. Frank Baum

The Wonderful Wizard of Oz

Chapter Nine

Carl pulled Grayson along the walkway into the city, where he inquired after pedicures at a salon. If they could come back in a couple of hours, there'd be slots free, and Carl snapped up the offer. "In the meantime, we can browse some shops, get something to eat."

They meandered their way quietly down a busy footpath and then Grayson ducked into a bustling bookstore. Not Carl's first choice, but anything if it picked up Grayson's spirits. While Grayson checked out novels of integrity, Carl ended up at a wall of magazines. Instinctively, he reached for one and froze as a sudden violent shudder ran through him. *Explains it all.* The memory of Green Gruff's words felt like a snigger in his ear.

Carl dropped his hand and shuffled backwards, banging into Grayson, who steadied him at the hips and glanced from Carl to the magazine. "Grab it if you want."

A sigh tried forcing its way out but Carl gulped it down. He pointed towards the exit and the street beyond. "I'm gonna check if there's space for us at that café over the road. Take your time."

Carl found a two-seater table at the window and stared glumly outside.

Then the sun came suddenly out from behind bubbly white clouds, beaming brightly on the street, casting it yellow. Through the bustle of pedestrians, Grayson's figure cut a clean path towards him. Though still in his sad grey, his tall frame, dark hair, and darker eyes made him difficult to ignore. He opened the door with a fresh rush of air, and a striking jolt jostled Carl. Like seeing someone he knew after a day with no customers at the store. A promise of interaction, and it crackled.

Carl waved him over, and Grayson seated himself, their knees knocking in the small space. He pulled a magazine from under his arm, and Carl recognised it as the one he'd refrained from checking out in the bookstore.

Carl kept glancing at it as they ordered coffee and food; Grayson watched him with that probing gaze that had Carl squirming and refilling his water.

"You're into horoscopes, right? You called me a Scorpio, there to stir stuff up?"

Carl fidgeted with a serviette in an effort to stop his fingers from snapping up the mag and checking it out. Only repeating Green Gruff in his head kept the urge at bay.

Grayson observed the shredded remains of the serviette and flipped open the magazine. "Let's look. What's your sign?"

Carl swallowed tightly. It was stupid to be so into this stuff. It wasn't like it was really real. Maybe if he spent more time reading actual books, he'd have better life prospects.

Grayson took out his phone. "You're twins. I'll just look up Jason—"

"You'd get it wrong. He was born before midnight; I was born after. We straddle the cusp of Sagittarius and Capricorn."

"Capricorn. Excellent."

"Wait, did you trick me?"

"You'll probably find it's a Scorpio trait. Let's see . . . ah, Capricorn—"

Carl plucked the magazine out of Grayson's hands and flipped to Scorpio instead. "We're both strong natured."

Their coffees and food arrived, and Grayson picked at his, waiting for Carl to diagnose him. His eyes were on him with a focused concentration that made Carl's skin prickle. One of the first sentences under Scorpio included "radiates intensity and crackles with charisma" and . . . check. But he'd leave that out—Grayson's ego didn't need *that much* stroking. It also said a Scorpio was hard to ignore, which . . . check again.

Smart. Check. *Shrewd.* Check. *Will always save the day.* Check.

"What's it say about me, hm?"

Carl cleared his throat and read. "*You don't switch off from work.* I've seen your calendar and this is painfully accurate. *You're a natural investigator. If there are secrets involved, so are you.* Well, seeing you've peeled me of mine, this also is true. *You're ceaselessly curious with an intensively calculating gaze to match.* Gosh, it's like this was written with you in mind. Ah, here we go: *Scorpio is most likely to form a cult.*"

"How is that—"

"Groupies."

"Go on."

Carl ate around a smirk and glanced at the list of Scorpio turn-offs: dull, stupid people—

He shut the magazine and slapped it on the edge of the table. "This food is delicious."

"So violently delicious?"

Carl prodded a fork in the air. "Stop looking at me like that."

"I'm a natural investigator. Ceaselessly curious—" Grayson stopped upon analysing the possibly trajectory of the water in the glass Carl lifted. "Okay, I'll drop it."

Carl sipped. "You know what's good for you."

After eating in silence for a few moments, Carl asked, "Did I drop stuff on my shirt somewhere? Why do you keep frowning at it?"

"Is it safe to answer?" Grayson said, eying Carl's water.

Carl folded his arms, and Grayson carried on, "You wore more flannel the first few times we met. Now you're in these tight and even tighter clothes."

"I've been trying to look more like Jason, so when he comes back others won't be too surprised."

"How comfortable are you in these clothes?"

Carl unfolded his arms and slouched in his chair. "They pinch a bit."

"Flannel's better, isn't it? What's most comfortable. What you actually *want* to be wearing."

Carl stared at Grayson and narrowed his eyes. "Are you saying things underneath things?"

"And you claim you're not clever."

Carl picked up one of his crusts, stuffed it in Grayson's mouth, and wagged a finger at him. "I promised I'd never stuff anything into your mouth again. But there's something about you that makes me want to break my word."

Grayson swallowed, gaze a sudden sparkle, and that sparkle mirrored itself low in Carl's stomach. "You promised this would be a two-way street, remember? You give advice. I give advice." He leaned in and said quietly, "Do you know that your eyes are scowling, but your lips are smiling?"

Carl couldn't stop the sparkles, dammit, but at least he could slap a hand over his smile. The scowl disappeared too. He was miffed at Grayson telling him it was better to be himself, and at the same time chuffed at the veiled praise of being clever. Also he was . . . Anyway, he could hold multiple feelings at once. Even if they did rattle about in his chest.

He flushed and motioned Grayson to finish eating. "Let's get moving."

~

CARL SANK INTO HIS PLUSH CHAIR WITH A RELAXED SIGH. Warm, bubbling scented water soaked their feet and gentle hands tended to each one, trimming and shaping and cutting away cuticles. His feet felt baby soft with all the moisturising, and he let out long, delighted moans. Grayson kept glancing at him, but other than asking for his toenails to be painted magenta, he didn't speak.

Not until the pedicurists had left, telling them to wait at least five minutes before putting on their shoes.

Carl murmured, "That was amazing. I love to be touched. Massaged."

"Everyone in here got that." Grayson cleared his throat, and it turned into a rather violent coughing fit.

Carl scooted off his chair and plunked himself beside Grayson, clapping his back. "You all right?"

Grayson nodded and ended up coughing again; Carl kept a hand roaming his wide back until he'd calmed.

"My cold is much better. Just had a strange tickle in my throat."

Carl rested his wrist on Grayson's shoulder and told him to wait a few more minutes before trying to leave. He looked at Grayson's cough-flushed cheeks and his gaze swept to his even redder ears, and there—Carl hadn't noticed before . . . He leaned in, gently touching Grayson's ear along the shell.

He trailed his fingers off the soft, scarred skin. He whispered softly at his ear, so they couldn't be overheard, "How did you get that?"

Grayson stilled next to him, a quiet sort of still, like he'd suspended his breath.

"Is this seat free?" A patron asked, gesturing to Carl's chair.

Grayson lurched to his feet so fast Carl tumbled onto the floor. By the time Carl had told the patron to go for it and picked himself up, Grayson was at the counter paying for the both of them.

"I wanted to get this," Carl said, coming up to him.

Grayson made for the exit sharpish. "Thanks for the foot afternoon. I've got . . . places to be. You know me, busy, busy."

"Whoa, hold on." Carl caught him by the sleeve outside and jostled him to the store wall to avoid being trampled. "I saw your calendar. You're wide open."

Grayson kept his eyes on the road and the buses coming down it. "I took work home to finish."

"Then consider me your PA today. I'll help."

"It's accounting stuff. You'd be better doing something else."

Carl grimaced. "Accounting."

"Lots of Excel sheets."

Ugh. Not his favourite. But, "I'll manage. For you."

Grayson shifted from foot to foot. "Okay, what is a ribbon and where does it appear?"

Carl scratched fingers through his hair. "On a . . . doll?"

"It's the main interface at the top of the Excel window allowing access to commands. What's pivoting? Dropdowns?"

"Shifting . . . onto your knees?"

"You'll be very bored." Grayson escaped between two groups of tourists towards the road. "You stay and have fun in town. I'll take the bus."

Carl frowned and watched as Grayson hurried across the road, slumped onto the bench at the bus stop, and ground his head against his palm.

Carl didn't chance upon Grayson for the rest of the day, or the following morning—despite a visit to Under The Raindough. Not that he had to be glued to the hip with him now that they were friends. It was just curious, since before, Grayson had haunted every other street corner.

"If being friends makes him disappear, I should have tried *that* at the beginning."

His musing was interrupted by the doorbell, and Carl started towards it at a sprint, only to slow to a crawl when he realised who it would actually be. He fished out his phone and texted Grayson.

Have that piano lesson!!! Help. Help.

The message was immediately marked as read, but Grayson was not typing back. Carl heaved out a sad sigh and managed to make it to the door.

It was hard not to regain his spirits when bright-eyed Leo bubbled his way into the house holding up all his music books. "Oh wow, Jason! Look at all these awards. Amazing. I can't believe you're letting me touch your grand piano!"

Carl ushered him to the impressive instrument and told Leo to go ahead and "feel the magic of the ivory under your fingertips. Absorb the power of the keys."

Grayson was right. He was fairly good at bullshitting.

"What's our first lesson?" Leo asked eagerly.

Carl glanced from the boy on the stool to the books he'd brought with him. "Of course, today is about gauging where you're at. If you'll play one of the pieces you know, I'll observe. See what good habits you have, and what ones need training out of you."

"Minuet in F Major?"

"Minuet," What on earth was a minuet? Could he possibly sweat more? "Excellent choice."

Leo played, and Carl nodded soberly and jotted things on a notepad that were remarkably like Scorpio traits and compatibility, pondering Grayson's encouragement to read his horoscopes if he liked them and wear flannel if he was more comfortable . . .

He scribbled them out and grimaced. The other times he'd played Jason, there'd been the fear of getting caught, yes, but the experience had also been energising. Praise scattered his way made him feel confident, seen. But today . . . Today playing Jason only felt stressful. "Ah, um, play a few more."

Leo did, and when the clock struck half the hour, Carl's perspiration had practically made a puddle on the floor. "We'll stop there for today."

"What do your notes say? Is it bad?"

Carl shook his head. "It's clear you love music and that shows in your playing. I hope you keep your enthusiasm, it helps when you have to perform a piece that you might not be as comfortable with."

Leo nodded. "What will we do next lesson?"

"Wait and see. Playing the piano takes much patience. Consider this practice."

"Sure! Mum asked if you could pop by the bakery after we'd finished?"

"Lead the way, Master Leo."

Carl followed Leo to the bakery with heavy steps. His original intention had been to help Leo against his bullies, but did going this far make *Carl* the bully?

Carl gulped. He needed to get out of any more fake lessons. The last thing he ever wanted was to cause anyone pain.

"Leo," Carl said thickly. "You remember how I said I was stupid—"

"Look, Grayson's here." Leo ran into the bakery.

Carl let out a deep breath, entered after Leo and, seeing him happily chatting to Grayson who was typing on his laptop in the corner, veered to the counter for Sage.

Sage brightened. "Thanks for popping by. I wanted to ask you over for dinner tonight. You'll come, won't you? Please?"

"Sure." How could he say no to such big, puppy-dog eyes?

Sage called over Carl's shoulder. "You want to come too?"

"I'm . . . good," Grayson said.

Leo batted his puppy-dog eyes and Grayson scrubbed the shadow forming on his jaw.

Sage added, "I really want to thank you both for helping so much with Leo."

Of course Grayson helped with Leo too. Probably tutored him in computer studies. Or showed him how to write a CV.

Carl glanced at Grayson, who kept staring at his computer screen while saying, "It's no biggie. I don't need thanking."

"Please? Please come."

Grayson started packing up his things, avoiding looking their way. What was up with him?

"Sorry, I'm booked up tonight." He checked his phone. "Gotta run." He waved to Leo and battled a few chairs on his way to the door.

Sage tutted. "Then let's *us* have dinner together," she said.

"Should I bring anything?"

"Just yourself. You're single right?"

"Huh?"

"My cousin Poppy—actually Alex, but everyone calls him Poppy—has been wanting to come round for dinner for a while. Can I invite him too? Maybe you'll hit it off."

Chair legs skidded over the floor and Carl jerked his head towards Grayson, suddenly back and searching the floor for . . . something he left behind?

Sage looked at Carl, waiting for an answer. "Oh. I'm recovering from a breakup."

"So sorry. When did that happen?"

"About a year ago."

"A year! Well then isn't it time to dip your feet back into the dating pool?"

"Um . . ." He was here to nurse his heart back to health, not bash it about some more.

"Even if it's just for a fling."

Fling.

The word hit him with a strange giddy plummeting. Of course he was put off ever falling in love again, but . . . a fling. Giving in to desire. Having fun . . .

There was something weirdly liberating in Sage's suggestion. Enjoying a moment. Sex. It wasn't like he *couldn't.* "I mean, I *am* single . . ."

Another chair protested against floorboards as Grayson, much slower this time, made his way back to the door.

"It's a date then," Sage said, clapping.

"Not a date."

"No, no, you'll only meet him. He'll be totally into you, though. You're his type."

The door shut loudly, startling Sage and Leo. And Carl murmured, "Gosh, the wind in Wellington is really something."

He stayed another few minutes enjoying a coffee at the bakery, and then made the two-minute trek home, where he found Grayson outside his gate holding a bike.

"Thought you were busy," Carl said, crossing to him.

Grayson's gaze was darker under the shadows of his helmet and it hit Carl with a zap. "Client's sick, they cancelled. Got time for a bike ride?"

Carl grabbed Jason's bike, jammed Toto on his head, and told Grayson to lead the way. They pedalled leisurely down to the beach and along the coast under a warm, curiously calm sky.

He breathed in the scent of salt water and almost felt the crashing of the waves against the rocks. Seagulls squawked overhead and their bikes hummed. A few small boats dotted shimmery turquoise-and-navy water, and Grayson riding ahead looked like he was in a scene from a movie.

Carl enjoyed the view. So much, he careened into Grayson's back wheel when he halted at a cosy, quiet beach not too far from where surfer Grayson had saved Jason's bike from pre-teen thugs.

Carl clambered off his bike and helped Grayson pick up his. They locked them up together, and set off down some stairs to the soft sand. Carl immediately kicked off his shoes, tied them together and draped them over his shoulders. He sank his feet into the warm, yellow sand. Grayson did the same, and pointed towards a driftwood log where they could sit.

Side-eyeing Grayson, Carl said, "You ignored my messages for help."

"You seem very capable of finding roundabouts." They seated themselves on the short driftwood, arms and legs barely a seashell apart.

Carl's phone buzzed in his pocket, and he checked the message. "Look, Sage sent a picture of her cousin. He . . . really pops."

Grayson's head bowed close to Carl's as he peeked at the screen. "Used a filter for sure."

"Good jawline. Kind-looking eyes."

Grayson had his judgy eyes riveted to Poppy's face. "Plain."

"Don't worry," Carl murmured, "he doesn't have to do it for you."

"That one picture is enough to have your heart thumping again?"

"For a fling, I'm . . .curious." Carl looked at Grayson and admitted something he'd barely let himself think. "Do you think . . ."

"Do I think, what?"

"I was sure I'd say no to Sage when she first suggested meeting Poppy. I mean, I'm here to heal, not . . . But a fling sounds safe. Doesn't have to mean more. And yet . . ."

Grayson drew in a breath. "Yet?"

"Am I using 'fling' as an excuse? Do I actually want to do this as an act of moving on? Am I after proof that passion can spark again?" Carl hummed. "Am I getting over my ex?"

Grayson swallowed and prodded a blunt-tipped finger at his phone. "With this guy?"

Carl sighed. "You sound extremely disbelieving. I get it, your heart's not quite ready to move on. It will, though. One day, you'll meet someone and they'll jumpstart that heart of yours. Maybe quite suddenly."

"Suddenly," Grayson repeated tightly and kicked a spray of sand towards the water as he laughed hollowly. "Is this photo your 'suddenly'?"

"In any case, some flirting over dinner might make me more confident that I'm close to a suddenly. Hmm, what should I wear?"

"It'll be colder at night and Sage doesn't often use her heat pump. Heap a few jerseys on. Puff yourself up."

"That might not look attractive."

"Even better. That way if you hit it off, you'll know it's not solely for your looks."

"But for a fling, isn't looks an essential part?"

"If it's a fling for a confidence boost, you'll be more empowered if he enjoys you with *all* your layers on."

Grayson had a point. He'd feel far more confident in himself and ready for a relationship if he knew his personality was as attractive as his face. "You might be onto something."

"I have a jacket made out of an old sleeping bag you could use. Made it for my mum when I was at intermediate school."

"I think I saw it alongside your tap shoes. I'll figure it out."

"You're really considering a fling?"

Carl bumped his shoulder against Grayson's. "And here's a bonus: you'll finally stop thinking I'm after you."

Grayson folded his arms and scoffed. "Or you're trying to make me jealous."

Light, ticklish laughter burst out of Carl. "You really are an adorable narcissist." He jumped to his feet, pulled Grayson off the driftwood and raced with him to the water, where a wave raced over their feet—a mighty cold bite that had Carl laugh-swearing. Grayson was used to it and cheekily kicked water over Carl.

That's it, game on. Grayson was much too quick for Carl to spray though, and it was him who ended up drenched. They made their way back to their bikes, sand caking their feet. "That felt good," Carl said. "I was starting to feel nervous about dinner but that helped. Thanks."

"You? Nervous?" Grayson said. "I find you very forthright."

"With you it's different. Tonight, I'll be flirting with a *man.*"

"What on earth does that make me?" Grayson grumbled.

Carl snuck up the stairs in front of him and patted his head. "You look like a dog who lost its favourite toy."

Grayson pretended to bite Carl's hand as Carl yanked it back, laughing. "I know it's hard to accept that not everyone is in love with you—"

Carl's heel banged into the step and he started to fall backwards. Grayson shot out his arms and caught him around his shoulders, but the angle was off and the balance just not there. In a tumble they landed against the stairs, Grayson draped over Carl.

Carl blinked, and laughed over a river of shivers.

A fling with someone he didn't know was digestible. Safe.

There was nothing safe about a fling with a friend. Especially when that friend was a renowned heartbreaker.

Grayson was a warm pressure against his vibrating body,

and it spurred Carl's incessant laughter on. He puffed each bout into the sea-salted crevice of Grayson's neck.

Carl wouldn't be that stupid. He'd continue to ignore all these bouts of electrical sizzliness. He'd absolutely slap himself silly if . . .

He'd never become a groupie.

A shiver rolled through Grayson, and the echo of it halted Carl's laughter.

Grayson finally found purchase on the steps either side of Carl and pushed up on his arms, taking the weight off Carl's chest. He stared down at Carl's face with big dark eyes, and Carl reached up and pinched his cheek. "We keep falling."

Grayson stared, and ripped himself off Carl. "The time. I've got to get to my next gig."

With that, Grayson raced up the stairs and freed his bike; by the time Carl had dusted himself free of sand and climbed to the road, Grayson was a grey spot rounding a curve in the distance.

"Run fast, and get out of this deadly flower bed as soon as you can."

L. Frank Baum

The Wonderful Wizard of Oz

Chapter Ten

Sage welcomed Carl into her pleasantly warm—much too warm for layers—home for dinner. He stripped off to Jason's t-shirt, draped his pullovers over a clothes hook in the hallway, and let Leo haul him to the lamp-lit lounge across from the dining room. There, the face from the photo sat in real life.

He was perched on a plush couch, the warm light from a nearby lamp glowing over his straw-coloured hair. He looked up as Carl entered, features chiselled, jaw strong, eyes gentle and curious. He was dressed in casual jeans and a stylish polo shirt. Neatly pressed yet at ease, comfortable. All in all, rather charming.

Carl smiled at him. "You must be Poppy?"

Sage called for Leo to 'help her a minute' and Leo ran off.

"She's leaving us right to it," Poppy said, smirking.

Carl dropped himself into the adjacent armchair. "She wants to see if we spark."

"What's your first impression?"

"Well, I now know you didn't use a filter on your photo."

"She sent you my photo?"

"How well do you know your cousin?"

Poppy laughed. "Of course she'd have done that."

The doorbell rang; Carl overheard Sage wondering who it was as she padded down the hallway, and Leo came into the lounge with sparkling water. Over the clinking of ice in the glasses, he heard muffled voices and Sage laughing cheerfully.

"Tell me, Jason, what do you do?"

Carl snapped his attention back to smiling Poppy and sipped his cool water. "Can we agree to talk about anything but work?"

Poppy chuckled. "I feel you. Agreed. What are your thoughts on—"

Whatever Poppy wanted to ask got lost as Grayson strode into the living room. There was an immediate shift in the air, something more than Carl's baffled lean in his direction. Poppy seemed to be stunned too, and fair enough. Not only had Grayson decided to come to dinner after all, he'd come in style. Black jeans moulded to his frame and a crisp white shirt that sat perfectly on his broad shoulders, top button casually open. His dark hair was impeccable, framing a cleanly shaven face, and his eyes hit them both hard. Carl was still breathing through the punch when Grayson swung his gaze to Poppy.

Sage scurried in behind him. "We're all here. You know Poppy."

"I do." The glare that came with that was . . . quite something. Possibly part of the reason he'd failed to mention it earlier?

Sage eyed them and quickly suggested they all move to the dining room.

The dinner table was set with bright plates and bone-handled cutlery on funky native-bird placemats. A big red pot was the centrepiece; crispy bread and a bowl of salad flanked it.

The lighting was brighter in here, and Carl couldn't shake

the feeling as he sat across from Poppy that Grayson—seated adjacent to them both—was running some kind of silent interrogation.

Carl shook it off and thanked Sage for inviting him for this lovely dinner as she spooned meaty stew onto their plates. She smiled and looked at them all. "I'll need your honest opinion on the food. I confess, I'm using you as guinea pigs."

"Guinea pigs?" Poppy asked, grinning.

It was a pretty nice grin but wow, *Grayson* didn't seem to think so. Not if his curled lip and judgy eyes were anything to go by.

Carl kicked Grayson's foot under the table, making the guy swing his intense gaze his way. "What're you doing?" Carl mouthed.

Grayson opened his mouth to say something, but took his steaming bowl from Sage instead. "What are we testing for?"

"The mums on the school board have asked me to join their fundraising team for the talent show."

"More like forced you," Leo grumbled.

"Hush. I've always wanted to be invited to help with these events. They're always at capacity though. This year they finally let me in. I'll be in charge of the food—I thought stew and fresh bread might be a winner?"

Carl and Poppy dipped their spoons into the stew and tasted, humming. "It's excellent."

"Taste's great!"

Grayson and Leo slicked on disapproving grimaces without so much as a taste. Grayson said, "They're asking you to donate everything?"

"Mostly it'll be cupcakes from the bakery."

"When did they ask you to volunteer?"

"At the Street Greet."

"Last minute? To donate *all* the food? They're exploiting you."

"I'm sure it's not like that," Sage said kindly. "They even said Leo and I could join the team-building session. A fun time at some escape rooms."

Leo frowned. "You *want* to go? I asked if we could do one last year and you said it was the last thing you'd ever want to do. Too many riddles."

Sage flushed and waved it off. "The mums said if it was too much, I didn't have to go to that. But you know, the offer was made."

"What an offer," Grayson bit out, and Carl was starting to feel why he was so upset. These witches seemed indeed to be using Sage, knowing how much she wanted to contribute and be included, making her donate a lot of costly food, and 'offering' a chance to join the team-building, betting that she wouldn't come.

"I'll go with you," Grayson said and held up his hand to stop any protests. "I'll pay for my own ticket. Besides, those mums are always calling me for favours even when I have other plans." He looked regretfully towards Carl, and Carl recalled the quiz night—having to stand in Grayson's place. "They owe me."

"What does the event raise money for?" Poppy asked with a winsome smile to everyone at the table, ending and lingering on Carl. "I'd be happy to donate."

"The funds go towards a new school pool."

"Mum, can I have more meat?" Leo asked.

"Sure, sure. Eat up everyone, before my bottomless pit here beats you all to it."

As they refocused on their stew, Carl felt eyes on him from Poppy's side of the table and glanced up to find he was right. He swallowed his mouthful. "Where abouts do you live?"

"Kelburn, up on the hills. Beautiful view." Poppy leaned in. "I could show you sometime."

Grayson grabbed a stick of bread and ripped into it so hard Carl felt the table jostle.

He forced himself to concentrate on the man across from him. "You've always lived in Wellington?"

"Best city in the world. Don't you think?"

"There are some wonderful views," Carl said, gaze skipping briefly to Grayson, who kept stuffing bread into his mouth.

So violently delicious? he wanted to ask.

Carl smirked around another swallow of stew.

"Could you pass me the salt?" Poppy asked, snapping Carl's attention back to him. Right.

Carl held out the salt grinder for him, and Poppy's hand closed around it, touching Carl's fingers warmly. Carl shot his head up, meeting a sparkly smile—

A third hand swiped the salt from the bottom, and Grayson began grinding over his bowl. "May as well circle it around," he said, smiling from Carl to Poppy and back again as he continued to grind.

Finally, with a good plunk, Grayson set the salt next to Poppy and spooned stew into his mouth. His face froze.

"Too much salt?" Sage called down the table. She and Leo had been eyeing the whole interaction and Sage seemed to find it most entertaining. Her eyes glittered bright blue under her strawberry blonde hair.

Grayson shovelled three spoonfuls into his mouth. His voice rose in pitch as he declared, "Exactly how I like it."

Sage's eyebrow started to come up, much like Carl's own, and Grayson pointed his spoon at Leo. "How was your day?"

"Great. Had my first lesson. Jason's piano is *grand*!" Leo giggled at his joke and gazed admiringly towards Carl. "There's a talent show at the school holiday charity event. A bunch of kids have signed up. I didn't think I should, but . . ."

Sage gasped. "You'd really perform in front of a crowd? I

thought the idea gave you stomach cramps. Remember those boys will be performing too."

"I always chicken out because I'm too scared. I know I might get laughed at, and I know those boys always win. But" —Leo took a deep breath—"Jason said we need courage to live our dreams."

"You're right, you're right!" Sage gave Carl the biggest, most thankful smile. "Such a motivating speech!" She looked back to her son, pride filling her eyes. "You'll really do it?"

Big, pleading eyes suctioned onto Carl's. "If Jason will help me? Tell me how to improve?"

So much hope drilled into Carl his throat seized up with the pressure of it. On a practical level, there wasn't much he could do to actually help. He also felt guilty that Leo and Sage really believed he could. But alongside the guilt was a feeling of massively blooming responsibility. He'd made Leo feel like he could be brave enough to go on stage against his bullies. To take that pillar of new-found courage away from him . . . that seemed as bad—worse, perhaps—as the lies.

Carl grabbed his water glass and gulped, stealing a glance at Grayson who gnawed his bottom lip, eyes pensively dark, like he couldn't work out the best response either.

"I'd love to support you being brave," Carl finally said. *That* was whole-hearted and true.

Leo leapt out of his chair with a fist in the air. "Can I come around again tomorrow and you help me pick a piece to play?"

Carl nodded under a stiff smile and hurriedly bowed his head towards his food.

"You're a musician?" Poppy murmured, gaze roaming over him with even more interest. "Maybe you can play on my instrument."

Grayson's glass tipped over, ice and water rushing across the table and into Poppy's lap, causing Poppy to squeal and jerk to his feet.

He flicked water off himself and glared at Grayson, then his glare steadied into something contemplative. "Huh." He smiled suddenly. "Never mind. Pants are removable."

Carl's gaze sank to Poppy's soaked lap, and suddenly Grayson was whirling Carl out of his chair and into the kitchen. "We'll clean up and help with dessert."

Grayson snapped on rubber gloves and started piling boards and knives and wooden spoons into the sink. Carl found a tea towel and dried things as they came out coated in suds.

"Why'd you decide to come to dinner?"

"I shouldn't have. I told myself not to."

"You told yourself not to?"

Grayson turned on the taps again. It took him a while before he answered. "Ah, because I have so much on." He prodded the mass of bubbles. "But I couldn't help it—Sage and Leo are always so much fun to hang with."

Carl stepped closer and was about to ask Grayson's thoughts on the Leo situation when Poppy came through with a stack of bowls.

"Let me help."

He took the tea towel from Carl and inserted himself between them. No chance of a private word with Grayson after that. Not during dessert, not before or after Leo went to bed, not while they capped the evening off with a brandy.

"Sage," Poppy murmured from the couch where he reclined comfortably in shorts borrowed from Sage. "Do you mind me crashing here tonight?"

"Course not."

Poppy's gaze cut to Carl. "Maybe I'll see you around tomorrow morning?"

Grayson pushed out of his armchair, thanking Sage for dinner. "Time to head off." He looked at Carl. "Shall we leave our host to it?"

At the door, Carl put all his layers back on, and outside—

door shut behind them—Grayson added his scarf. "*That's* how puffed up you should've come."

"What's with you tonight? You're acting . . . off."

Grayson marched through the gate, turned down the footpath and threw Carl a look. "He kept ogling you."

"Ogling me."

"That t-shirt's very clingy and your jeans are outrageous."

"What's wrong with them? Other than the pinching."

"You looked like you wanted to be ravished there and then."

"I did not."

"You absolutely did."

"What's the problem if I did look . . . ravishing?"

"You wanted to boost *Carl*'s confidence. Not Jason's."

"Is that why you were weird all evening?"

Grayson jerked his head away; his throat jutted with a deep swallow. "Didn't we agree to be friends? A good friend would look out for you. The real you."

The real him.

In the quiet of the night, under the soft glow of a streetlamp, those words fluttered in Carl's stomach.

He stepped forwards and Grayson's body tightened, but he moved his head to fix a gut-punching gaze on Carl. Deep, thoughtful—and as he claimed, protective.

Air shifted and leaves rustled, and abruptly, Grayson stepped back. "I'm surfing tomorrow. Early." He narrowed his eyes at Sage's house and then looked over at Carl. "Did you want to come?"

Carl didn't have much experience surfing—and neither did Jason, judging by the lack of wetsuit in his wardrobe. Despite not having gear, Carl was strangely eager to go.

He shook off little electrical zaps, putting them firmly away in the 'Ignore' column of his brain, and focused on the nature, the fresh air, and the early morning.

He jumped into Grayson's idling ute and handed over a travel cup of steaming coffee. "I love that we're early birds."

Grayson took the offered cup with a glance at Carl's lap and a raised brow. "Because of catching worms?"

Heat flooded Carl's cheeks and he groaned. "You're going to hold that untimely fall against me forever, aren't you?"

Grayson laughed. "My groupies go to such lengths, the least I can do is appreciate their efforts."

Carl swatted Grayson's arm. "Take that back."

"I really don't want to."

"It's a wonder your head isn't twice as big."

They were the first to arrive at Houghton Bay, and the cool sand beneath Carl's bare feet sent happy shivers through him. Dawn painted the sky in strong strokes of rippling pink, and beyond the ragged, rocky coastline was a stunning view across Cook Strait to the South Island's mountainous peaks.

Stripped down to his wetsuit, Grayson hefted his surfboard under one arm and admired the view. "The day you lost your bike, a pod of dolphins visited the bay. Saw orcas here once too."

"At home we've got tiger snakes and giant huntsman spiders."

"Really selling it, Carl. Take me there right now."

Carl laughed. "Actually it's alright. A lot of Victorian architecture—quaint cottages and colourful gardens. The town square has a fountain and a historic clock that's always malfunctioning. There's a public park and a walkway that winds around the town, a police station I'm overly familiar with, and the best wee convenience store around. Every morning the scent of fresh donuts has the locals streaming in for their filter coffee and a good ol' chat. It's the heart of all the gossip, and I'm pretty much at the centre of it."

"Perfect for someone who loves to meddle."

"I don't *meddle*—" At Grayson's arched brow, Carl relented. "Yeah, okay."

"It sounds cosy."

Carl hummed dreamily as they stared towards the horizon and the nice surfing swells rushing to shore. After a moment, Carl gestured for Grayson to head in. "I'll sit and enjoy the view."

"No doubt," Grayson said.

Carl kicked up a spray of sand and Grayson dodged it, racing into the frigid water with his board.

From a sturdy log, Carl breathed in the salty air and smiled. The vast sky, the ragged hills, the wide-open sea. What more was there to enjoy on this early morning—

Wow. Grayson!

Carl sat straighter, keenly watching his every move. How smoothly he mounted his board, the harmony he had with the ocean . . . Wave after wave he caught with grace and style, and as the sun rose higher, his athletic figure zipped along the golden water and rode all the way to shore.

Carl choked on a hoppy-electric laugh as Grayson emerged from the water. Seriously? He looked like he was putting on a show—or acting in one.

He *shimmered* from the surf. Water dripped from his wetsuit, ran down his ridiculously chiselled face from hair that clung in tendrils around it. He shook his head and light hit the droplets that sprayed around him, making them glisten like crystals.

Carl shook his head in horrified amazement. Life had to be shitting him right now. No way were people this glorious in real life. This looked staged.

Carl couldn't help darting his head around.

He didn't spot any cameras, but he did spot two familiar

figures jogging down the steps to the beach. His old high-school mates, now successful lawyers and general winners at life.

His stomach sank. Hurriedly, he shielded his flushing face with a splayed hand.

Grayson grabbed his yellow towel from beside Carl and scrubbed his hair, eyeing him. “What are you doing?”

“Shh.” Carl grabbed Grayson by a wet knee and steered him closer, hopefully blocking himself from view. He peeked around Grayson’s thigh.

“Who are you hiding from?” Grayson murmured from above.

Carl glanced up at his curious, somewhat bemused expression, and beckoned him closer with four curling fingers. Grayson leaned down and drops from his hair pattered over Carl’s face. “I *can’t* with them.”

Grayson shuffled and crouched, a barrier between Carl and Classmates.

“They think I’m an uneducated bum stuck in my small town with no prospects.”

A heavy growl had Carl snapping his gaze away from impending discovery to Grayson’s very pink and very pinched lips. He looked about ready to whirl around and confront the fellows and Carl grabbed his wrist to keep him close. “That’s what I took from subtext. They didn’t say anything outright.”

“You got all that from subtext?”

“They paid for my lunch.”

Grayson cocked his head and repeated softly. “They paid for your lunch?”

Carl squeezed Grayson’s wrist. “It was the *way* they paid for it.”

A hand landed atop Carl’s. “It’s enough if you felt down after seeing them.”

Carl looked into Grayson’s determined gaze and once

again his belly fluttered . . . "Ugh, they're coming our way." Eventually there wouldn't be enough Grayson to hide him from view.

He squeezed his eyes shut and prepared for some awkward conversation—

A damp towel landed over his head.

Carl opened his eyes and blinked. Grayson was holding his towel over both of them like they were in a secret blanket fort. Sunlight filtered through the yellow fabric in a warm glow, and their breaths mingled in the sudden tight space.

Dark eyes stayed on Carl, warm and understanding, with that signature hint of mischief. Like he genuinely wanted to help, but also found the situation somewhat amusing and wanted to tease him. It made it difficult to know how to respond. Squeeze his wrist tightly until that slight smirk disappeared? Or squeeze him gently with a mouthed 'thank you'?

Carl squeezed midway between tight and gentle and felt Grayson's pulse ticking under his fingers. The rhythmic beat against him while they sat so close made Carl's squeeze feel . . . intense. He could see the trace of stubble along Grayson's strong jawline.

A moment of brighter sunshine illuminated Grayson's expression—his darkening eyes, his fading smile—

Too much!

Carl ripped his hand away and brought the towel crashing down between them. That was not intended to be a romantic squeeze. Now Grayson would never believe he wasn't interested.

If *that* wasn't enough to have his heart pounding, his old classmate-lawyers had crossed the beach and were within inevitable spotting distance . . .

Their heads lifted . . .

They glanced at him—

And looked hurriedly away again.

One pointed towards the water, as if they'd seen something worthy of their attention, and they angled themselves away from Carl towards it. As if . . . they didn't want Carl to spot *them*.

That . . . should be fine. Carl hadn't wanted to be spotted, either.

But . . .

His stomach dove and his throat tightened. He shoved to his feet and stumbled over the sand in his hurry to get to Grayson's ute, and once he was inside, he pressed his forehead against the glass and let it rattle through him as they drove silently back to Berhampore.

"Carl . . ."

"Don't."

"You promised we were a two-way street."

Carl swallowed and continued staring out the window at the houses and the hills flashing by.

Grayson murmured, "Those guys hurt you. It must've made you feel shitty, seeing them again."

Carl's chest ached. "It's not really them. I barely know those two. It's that . . . recently I feel like I'm not . . . interesting enough? Don't have enough to offer?" He laughed hollowly and swiped at a sting in his eyes. "If I'm a magazine, I've got no journalistic integrity."

Grayson pulled to a stop at Jason's place, and their pensive breaths thickened the air between them. Carl picked at his blunt fingernails and felt his cheeks and throat burn as Grayson observed him. "I can imagine feeling like that makes you feel lonely."

A violent hiccup raced through Carl and forcing it back down hurt his throat. "We talked about getting a dog and I was stupidly happy to be giving him a kennel, but what's a kennel to free vet care?"

Grayson couldn't know what Carl was on about, but he listened patiently.

Carl shoved a hand through his hair. "My ex, he fell in love with a veterinarian. He was mesmerised by how incredible he was, how smart. And the thing is, Nick really is a decent guy. I get why Pete chose him."

"Wait a sec. Falling for someone has no intelligence measurement like that. It happens if there's a connection. Doesn't matter what the person does for a job as long as there's this strange spark between them. Even if they don't want it and tell themselves it's crazy and they're not ready—they fall anyway."

Carl breathed in, frowning gently. That was all comforting and hopeful, but he wasn't entirely sure his life choices didn't play a role in Pete's decision.

Grayson seemed to sense Carl still needed convincing. He gripped the steering wheel and continued, "I might meet the most intelligent and accomplished person, and still be bored by them; put to sleep after half a conversation. Exhausted from forcing myself to keep up." His fingers started a soft drum over the wheel and he glanced towards Jason's house, swallowing. "Or, I might meet a kind person who enjoys bike rides and hikes and likes to be up early in the morning, and never feel bored."

Carl . . . got that. If some guy struck up a conversation on, like, intricate details of the middle to late Byzantine period, he'd totally start a smile-and-nod routine while mentally working out his shopping list for the upcoming week. So maybe it made sense that intelligence didn't equal being worthy of attraction?

Thinking it through like this . . . helped. A chunk of the silly weight on his chest came off and he could breathe a little easier. Carl wagged his finger. "This two-way street thing is gold."

Grayson's lips twitched.

Carl felt his own tick up too.

"I've got a job to get to, but . . ." Grayson stared into the middle distance, as if struck by a thought, then grimaced and nodded to himself. "What will you do the rest of the day?"

"Leo's coming round later. That's a whole other conversation—"

A groan-chuckle. "Not right now."

A sighing laugh seeped out of Carl as he tried and failed to get his belt to open. Grayson reached over and freed him, their thumbs grazing on the buckle with a static jump. They quickly pulled apart and he clambered out of the car. "Do something fun for yourself," Grayson said after clearing his throat. "Something distracting."

He looked over at Grayson with a smile before he shut the door. "I will. Promise."

I shall take the heart, for brains do not make one happy, and happiness is the best thing in the world.

L. Frank Baum

The Wonderful Wizard of Oz

Chapter Eleven

Carl held true to his promise to distract himself, even if only by accident. When he bumped into Possible-Fling-Poppy outside the bakery, particularly hungry after the trip to the beach, Carl thought food sounded like a solid idea.

They went to the eatery across from Under The Rain-dough, sat at an outside table next to grey tussock in planter boxes, and ordered breakfast tacos for the table off an iPad.

The iPad shifted from ordering mode into five-second-trivia-question-and-answer mode—something to inspire conversation, perhaps—but Carl stared grimly at it.

Poppy misinterpreted his glare for uncertainty, glanced at the question—where is Matiu located—and answered before going on to share other te reo Māori names for areas in Wellington.

As he bit into his first taco, Carl caught sight of Grayson whizzing past on his bike and around the corner towards Jason's villa. Was he due to mow more lawns around there? Or was he heading back to visit?

Carl frowned and shook himself back to the conversation that'd somehow jumped to New Zealand's Great Walks.

Another trivia question perhaps? Carl heard as much as 'Abel Tasman', then spied Grayson pushing his bike back from Carl's road.

Returning so soon and slightly deflated like that . . . could it mean he had wanted to see Carl?

Something warm fluttered in Carl's stomach. He sat straighter and waved to catch Grayson's attention.

Grayson caught the movement, looked his way, and visibly paused with his bike for a few dark-gazed seconds before he continued towards them.

The table rattled as Carl leapt to his feet. "Grayson!" He gestured to the spare seat at their table, "Join us."

Poppy sighed beside him and a look his way confirmed a grimace.

Grayson locked up his bike and seated himself, adjacent to Carl, opposite Poppy. The air suddenly tensed, and a muscle twitched in both their jaws.

The weirdness from last night returned. Did they have some kind of history? In the kitchen, Grayson had told Carl he shouldn't have come. That he'd told himself not to. *That he couldn't help it.*

Maybe . . .

But Grayson was Berhampore's heartbreaker. Had he broken Poppy's heart and that led to this strange atmosphere between them? Grayson had been rather dismissive of Poppy's photo at the beach.

But what did it mean that he 'couldn't help it'? Despite however they'd left things, did Grayson *like* Poppy?

Was the whole being protective thing an excuse to stop Carl and Poppy getting closer, because Grayson wasn't finished with him yet?

"What are you frowning for?" Grayson asked. Carl quickly threw together a taco and handed it to him.

"I thought you had work."

"I said I wasn't feeling so great. I'll make it up another time."

"You threw a sickie?"

Grayson looked at him, their gazes connecting. The softness in those pools of black had Carl's stomach jumping so hard he almost hiccupped.

"I had more important things to do today."

Don't think those important things are related to you. There could be plenty of things Grayson wanted to do. Perhaps after checking in on Carl at the villa, he'd always intended to catch Poppy . . .

Poppy cleared his throat, and Carl swung his head around to eyes that were suctioned intently on Grayson. Too intently. Like Poppy had unfinished business there too. Carl didn't like it.

He slapped together another taco. "Poppy," he said, drawing the man's attention away from Grayson. He smiled and placed the taco on Poppy's plate, then put his elbow on the table and propped his chin on it, cutting into some of Poppy's view of Grayson. He even fluttered puppy-dog eyes. "Taste good?"

Poppy smiled brightly and tried to fling Grayson another *look*; Carl intercepted with a hand reaching for the iPad of trivia. "History questions." He ignored the lurch in his stomach and continued distracting the two from intensely gazing at one another. "Who was the first human to travel into space?"

They answered simultaneously. "Yuri Gagarin."

"Wow," Carl murmured under his breath. These guys really had history. Light a match and something would start burning here.

"Bet I can answer five before you can," Poppy said, goading Grayson.

Grayson looked at Carl. "Go on."

Yay. Great. Wonderful. He'd intended to distract them from flirting and now he was conducting it.

He forced up a smile and surreptitiously jabbed the screen to 'difficult' questions.

"Poppy: In the fifteenth century BC, who was the first female pharaoh of ancient Egypt?"

"Hatshepsut."

"Grayson: Who was the first female physician in Japan, who made huge contributions to public health and education in the 19th and 20th centuries?"

"Ogino Ginko."

"Poppy: What Russian mystic and faith healer was advisor to the Romanov family and murdered in 1916?"

"Rasputin."

"Grayson: In 480BC, although vastly outnumbered, the Athenians defeated a Persian fleet and altered the course of the Greco-Persian Wars. What was the name of that battle?"

"The Battle of Salamis."

Their answers continued, quick and correct. Grayson got particularly obscure questions, to Carl's mind, and hadn't batted an eye before answering.

. . . "The Righteous and Harmonious Fists, known as the Boxers."

Carl blinked at him. *This* had to be why the Green Gruffs thought they'd win Quiz Night. Yikes.

A bubbly "Yoo-hoo" had all three of them jerking their gazes to Sage, hair tucked into a net; she jogged across the road to their table with a bright smile and a wave.

"I'm after a wee bit of help at the bakery, I wondered—"

"Helping? I love helping!" *Sage, you absolute saviour.* Get him away from this weird flirting. He jumped to his feet.

The two idiots either side of him did not take up the opportunity to bond one on one. They rose swiftly from their chairs. "Of course I'll help," Grayson said, while Poppy said, "Helping is my middle name."

"Wonderful," Sage exclaimed with a happy clap.

Poppy charged eagerly over the road with Sage; Grayson started a quick stride too, but Carl grabbed him by the elbow, holding him back. "Stay with me a sec."

Grayson, bless him, obliged immediately.

"I really have to thank you," Carl murmured.

"Thank me?"

"When you talked earlier in the ute about intellect not equalling attraction, it got me thinking maybe you had a point, and now—" he gestured to the table and the trivia still flashing on the iPad. "After that show. I *really* believe it."

Grayson rubbed a palm over his jaw. "Not even a little attraction?"

"God, no."

Carl headed across the road and after a moment Grayson moved as well, catching up beside him. "What would be attractive?"

"Good question. Not sure. But I'd be far more turned on by a guy showcasing some physical skill." The image of Grayson mowing the neighbour's yard shirtless flittered to mind. Carl gave himself a little slap on the cheek to keep his thoughts clear as Grayson got the door.

Inside, the bakery was empty of customers but full of delicious scents. One glance into the kitchen showed two tables of un-iced cupcakes. Poppy was leaning against the counter umming and ahhing over a tray of pink and blue frosted ones. Sage stood opposite him, gnawing on her bottom lip, and in the corner by the windows Leo was messing around on an iPad and hadn't noticed them come in.

Grayson sidled up to the counter beside Carl, and Carl groaned. Once again he'd become the third wheel between these two guys with history. He trained his gaze on Sage, who caught his eye with a nervous twinkle in her own. "I'm doing a practice run for the charity event. I wanted to make the cupcakes special to the occasion, but I'm not sure I like these."

Carl stared at the beautiful, classic-style cupcakes sprinkled with tiny silver balls.

"These look wonderful."

"I wouldn't waste your time trying to please those mothers," said Grayson.

Sage looked between them all and landed on Carl. "What do you think?"

Carl thought . . . he understood why it was important to Sage to prove to the witches she was worthy of being on the volunteer team. To show she had what it took, not for them to dismiss her abilities. For that, Sage wanted cupcakes that stood out. That said 'I can organise things as well as you can'. "What if they were iced in the school uniform colours? Green and yellow?"

"Ohhh, that would be brilliant," Poppy said immediately.

Even Grayson was nodding.

Carl side-eyed the two flanking him and shifted in the weird air between them. They seemed to be gazing in his direction, as if trying to see each other through him.

Before he could step back, Sage reached over the counter and clamped a hand on his shoulder. "Great idea. You. You'll be the ultimate judge." She swung her gaze between her cousin and Grayson. "You two, add colouring to the icing, fill the piping bags, and do three designs each. The winning one will be used for the event." She waved a hand at all the cupcakes behind her. "We can practice on these."

"That's an awful lot of practice," Carl murmured.

Sage grinned. "The volunteers and teachers will practice eating them for morning tea. Let's get this done." She laughed. "See which of you bakers is best."

"You bake as well?" Carl asked Poppy.

A slick smile tipped his lips. "I come from a family of bakers. I grew up icing cupcakes." Poppy threw Grayson quite the look of challenge. "I'm a master."

Grayson shoved up his sleeves and threw Poppy an apron, hairnet and gloves; Poppy caught them hard against his chest with a laugh.

Sage sidled around the counter to join Carl as the guys fussed around adding dye to the icing. She talked a steady stream into her phone—lists of ingredients, reminders of things to do that morning. At Carl's quizzical look, she showed him her screen of notes. "Voice to text. Saves time and typos."

Carl played around with it, speaking into the phone and watching his words appear on the screen. "That's kind of brilliant." He scrolled down the list Sage had curated and paused. "Uh, you have to deliver the cupcakes at the same time you have a doctor's appointment?"

She winced and plucked the phone from him. "I didn't put in a reminder." Her shoulders slumped and her nervous excitement fizzled. "Silly me. I wanted to take part in the meeting. Show I'm reliable. But I also really need that appointment . . ."

Carl felt his chest sort of puff up in sympathy. Here Sage was, doing her absolute best—totally able to pull this off—and now those witches would have the smug satisfaction of having their assumptions about her failings confirmed. That was . . . frustrating. It sparked in him the same kind of feelings as 'Dead End' did.

He banged a fist on the counter, making Sage's first cupcakes jump. "How long's your appointment? Where?"

"Fifteen minutes. It's always on time too, and just down the road. I'd only be 20 minutes late but those mums . . ."

"Let me help?"

"You would? How?"

"You'd have to set up the cupcakes in the hall kitchen first, right? I'll do that part, and I'll stall them from starting the meeting until twenty past."

"They'll wonder why I'm not in the kitchen."

"So you disappeared to the toilet for a minute. Or you're grabbing more cupcakes from the car. I could even . . ." Carl leaned in and whispered an idea in her ear.

Sage cracked up laughing. "You're kidding. You'd do that?"

"Why not?"

"You have to be one of the kindest guys I've ever met. To do that. For me?"

How happy this idea made her. Made Carl more eager to do it. "Then it's a deal?"

"I can help you pull it off if we head across to my place after this?"

Carl looked back into the kitchen at Poppy and Grayson facing off across a table as they pressed icing through bags onto their cupcakes. The tension was so thick he reckoned even the baker's knife would have trouble cutting through it. "We could go right now if you like?"

Sage laughed, tipping her chin up with delight. "They really are putting on a show, aren't they? Don't you find it amusing?"

Carl rubbed his jaw. "I don't understand the need to flex their insanely toned biceps like this. They're icing cupcakes."

Poppy blew dusted icing sugar off his bulging muscle towards them in a fine spray. Grayson's eyes narrowed hard on the show. That was . . . a lot of attention he was paying. An envious shiver rippled through Carl, despite telling himself it shouldn't matter.

He pinched himself to his senses and focused with all his might on their cupcakes—biceps—*cupcakes*!

Sage giggled. "I've got a feeling Poppy will win this."

Poppy smirked and threw them a wink.

"Win what?" The curious voice startled Carl and he

shifted, letting Leo squeeze between them. "Mum, you're so wrong. Grayson all the way."

"You're my favourite kid for a reason, Leo," Grayson said. His gaze slid to Carl's.

"Choose Grayson," Leo whispered, while Sage giggled and said, "Say Poppy."

"I think . . ." Carl snapped his gaze from Grayson to Poppy and back again. "I'll judge by the cupcakes. Come on then." Get this over and done with. "Show me what you've got."

With a twist and a swivel of their bags, they squeezed out icing and set the first cupcake before the three of them. Leo, of course, voted for Grayson's. Sage, Poppy's. Which left Carl with the deciding vote. The cupcakes were equally great. One green, one yellow, Poppy's with a chocolate swirl, and Grayson's with chocolate bits.

"Both have me drooling?" Carl said and the hopeful gazes riveted on Carl turned on each other with purpose. They dusted their gloved hands, rolled their shoulders, and raced to decorate the next.

These second cupcakes were outrageous. There was more icing than cupcake. Grayson used chocolate to draw stick figures of children around the edges, while Poppy drew waves, which Carl assumed was for the pool the donations would go towards.

The last cupcakes . . . took the cake. In fact, neither cupcake could be seen under the elaborate wedding-cake-esque icing arrangements. In Grayson's hands green icing had turned into intricate leaves upon which sat not one but three fully bloomed yellow flowers. Poppy's cupcake turned into a ball upon which a tiny icing pupil sat eating . . . a cupcake.

Carl couldn't help but rub his forehead as he stared at the insanity before him. *These guys are something else.*

He went right back to their first attempts and tapped his

finger before the plates. "Half like this and half like that. Pretty and practical."

"We both win?" Poppy said, disappointed.

Carl blinked between boys and baked goods. "Winning would be putting it optimistically."

A little laugh leapt out of Grayson and he straightened his hair net. "Let's get icing then."

Carl checked the time. They needed to work fast now. "I'm heading to Sage's place for a few minutes. Can you have them done by the time we get back?"

Carl had barely finished speaking before the next stage of this flirtation began. He couldn't get outside fast enough. He shook himself in a much welcome breeze. If he should ever behave so foolishly . . .

Like swapping lives with your twin and pretending to be him on multiple occasions? Or what you're about to do for Sage?

Okay, then.

These guys might in fact be his crowd. What was a little foolishness in the grand scheme of things?

He nodded to himself, followed Sage to her place, and quickly rummaged together the things he needed. When they returned to the bakery, it was to a flurry of movement as Poppy and Grayson competed to finish their last half-row of cupcakes.

Leo glanced at them and did a double take. "Mum? Jason? Why are you . . ."

Finally with a "Ha! I win" from Poppy, two other sets of eyes landed on them and blinked. Hard. Grayson set down his piping bag, wiped his hands on his silver apron, and slunk towards them, eyes roaming up and down Carl's length. "Why are you both wearing the same dress?"

Carl and Sage did a twirl showing off their identical wrap-around dresses. Carl's shorts and t-shirt fit nicely under it, which would make getting out of costume take a matter of seconds. "Poppy, throw us some hairnets?"

Sage added, "And face masks. There're some under the counter."

With the nets completely covering their hair and the face masks on, at a glance—and a glance was all that would be needed—they looked rather similar. They were even the same height.

"Is there a particular purpose for this getup?" Grayson asked, eyebrows still up around his hairline.

Carl snuck over to him and whispered in his ear. "Will you help me? If the mums ask where 'Sage' is, vaguely point in my direction and tell them I'll join the meeting in a jiffy?"

"If he won't help, I will," Poppy said, shooting a pick-me hand in the air.

Grayson grabbed the neck of Carl's wraparound dress and squared it neatly over his t-shirt. "I'm familiar with both the school and these mums. I'll do it. You hold the fort here with all your *baking experience*."

Leo kept looking between Carl and his laughing mum; Sage swatted him gently over the back of the head, turning it into a fond rub that had Carl swallowing.

He shook off the sudden tender longing, but not before Grayson caught a glimmer of it. He seemed to understand in a glance. Carl shot into the kitchen, in case Grayson murmured anything reasonable in his ear. He was in a volatile mood this morning, and he didn't want to appear any more foolish than he already was.

"Let's get this show on the road."

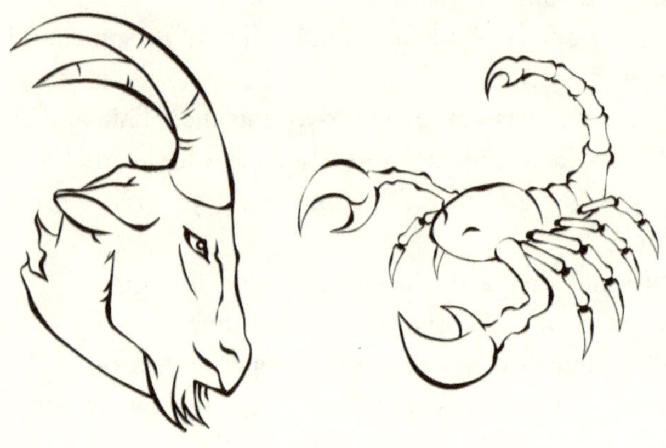

"But suppose we cannot?" said the girl.

"Then I shall never have courage," declared the Lion.

"And I shall never have brains," added the Scarecrow.

"And I shall never have a heart," spoke the Tin woodman.

"And I shall never see [home]," said Dorothy, beginning to cry.

L. Frank Baum

The Wonderful Wizard of Oz

Chapter Twelve

They transported the cupcakes in Sage's car, which certainly helped the disguise Carl was trying to pull off. On the two-minute ride, Carl side-eyed Grayson. "What was all that about? You and Poppy."

Grayson stared out the windscreen to the traffic light they'd stopped at. "He was competing against me. For your . . . approval."

It took Carl a few moments to process that. "All that was for *me*? *Why*? Did Sage tell him I'm one of your groupies? He got it all wrong. And *you*"—Carl banged a chastising fist against Grayson's upper arm—"You're mischievous, you know that?" Carl replayed the morning and laughed. "All those poor cupcakes. All to tease him."

"Teasing?" Grayson mumbled. "I was acting the part of jealous suitor."

Carl patted his shoulder with a nod. "You made him work for it. Good friend. I'll go see him once we're done here."

Grayson came to an abrupt halt inside the school gates. "You're going back to him?"

"To clarify it all." And turn him down gently. Even for a fling, Poppy didn't feel right.

Carl gazed at Grayson climbing out of the car. The grace. The gorgeousness—

He gave himself another sharp slap on the cheek.

"You all right?" Grayson asked.

"Bug." Love bug. *That he must squash immediately!*

Inside, bowed over three dozen cupcakes in the hall kitchen and only partially visible to the teachers and volunteer mums strolling in, they got the show on the road.

It was easier than he'd thought. Grayson, playing the role of Sage's helper, didn't even need to throw out the line about 'Sage' making her way into the main hall soon. The witches beat him to it.

"Sage is here already!"

"Must be eager to impress."

"Let her have her moment."

In fact, hearing that, *Carl* nearly gave them away. His head shot up, fury blazing in his eyes, and only Grayson whirling him into a dance saved the show. They twirled to the beat of Mariah Carey's "Almost Home" crackling over Grayson's phone until Carl calmed himself and folded into the steps, like Sage would've done. He couldn't stop glaring over Grayson's shoulder, though. And he held Grayson's hand so hard the heat was starting to make them stick.

Once the witches passed the kitchen, Carl stopped dancing and said in Grayson's ear. "Can I put laxatives on their cupcakes?"

Rumbling laughter vibrated through Carl, making him realise how snug he was against Grayson. His pulse kicked up a gear and a shiver slunk through him.

Hurriedly, he peeled himself away and turned back towards the plated cupcakes.

He checked the time. Already quarter past. Sage should

arrive in the next five to ten minutes, and to stall the meeting out there . . . He made sure no one could see him and quickly unwrapped the dress, pulled off his mask, and uncovered his hair. In an instant, he was Carl again. Correction: he was Jason Lyall.

"What are you doing?" Grayson said as Carl headed towards the main hall.

"Stalling. Sage wants to be properly involved. That means the meeting will start when she arrives. Bring the plates to the tables?"

"The piano—what if they pressure you to play?" Grayson cuffed Carl's bare wrist. "You're not wearing your bandage."

"This was a spontaneous thing. I didn't bring it."

The moment Grayson tugged Carl back into the kitchen, the scudding of chairs over the floor as staff and volunteer parents chatted in the main hall became a soft background hum.

Grayson opened drawers and cupboards, searching them swiftly, keeping a gentle grasp on him.

Carl stared at those careful fingers and wondered if Grayson felt the ticking of his pulse under them, like at the beach, under the towel. He waved his free hand in front of his face. Plenty more air in this kitchen, yet it felt similarly warm.

"You alright?" Grayson asked, spying his rapid face-fanning hand.

Carl dropped it to his side and mustered a nod.

Behind the cutlery tray was a clear bag of plasters, and Grayson snatched them up. "Stay right there."

Air funnelled around his fingers but the feel of Grayson's hand around Carl's stayed. He stared at it until suddenly Grayson was before him again, holding up a large plaster smothered in raspberry jam. Carefully, Grayson wrapped it around Carl's index finger, smoothing out a ruffled edge with the tip of his fingernail. The gentle scrape sparked a violent shiver, and Carl . . . liked it. He . . . didn't want to ignore it.

He slammed his eyes shut and shook his head. *Heartbreaker.*

"There," Grayson said. "Credibility."

A short sound had him reopening his eyes and spinning around to Leo, tucked behind the doorframe to the kitchen. He was frowning, perplexed. "What—"

"Leo!" Grayson said, aiming for cheerful and distracting. "Where did you come from?"

"I got bored at the bakery. Wanted to see if you needed help." Leo kept staring at Carl's plastered finger, and guilt sank Carl's stomach to his knees. This was it. He'd kept finding excuses not to come clean—there was always another feeling that trumped the truth—but now . . .

Leo flattened his lips, frown deepening.

The chatter from the hall had died down—the meeting was about to start. He really wanted to stall it on Sage's behalf, but faced with lying to help her or saving his friendship with Leo . . .

Carl turned to Grayson with a light, pleading touch to his arm. "I can't go in there."

Grayson's warm dark eyes held his with understanding. "Go on. I've got this."

With sluggish steps, Carl walked out into a fresh breeze with Leo. They didn't look at one another or say anything as they crossed the concrete quad, headed up a zigzag path and rounded a playground to a view of houses and hills. The grass was soft under them when they sat. Leo grabbed a stick and started stabbing it into the dirt.

Carl thought he probably deserved to be under that stick.

He sighed and unwrapped the plaster. "You saw Grayson smear jam on this, huh?"

A demanding look. "Why?"

"My gut tells me you already have an idea."

"You wore a bandage to assembly and couldn't perform. Now you're wearing jammed-up plasters. You don't want to play."

"Mm. I don't want to play."

"Because it's too much to ask? Or because we're not paying you? Or . . ." He stabbed the grass again.

"Finish that 'or'."

"*Or* you don't know how."

Carl ran a hand through his hair and stared out towards the forested hills. "I mean, I might be able to sound out Three Blind Mice . . ."

Leo dropped his stick and stared at him. "You're not a professional? Why did Mum think . . . why did you pretend you *were*?"

"Fair questions. Your mum was right. Jason Lyall is a famous pianist."

"You're not Jason Lyall? Oh my God. You're an evil twin?"

"Would we call me evil?"

"You're a twin?"

"And cowardly imposter."

Leo opened his mouth to say something and slammed it shut again. Instead, he blinked, and blinked again. "You pretended to be your twin? Does he know? Are there two of you walking about confusing us?"

Carl explained the situation. Swapping places with his brother was only meant to be for a few weeks. Carl wasn't supposed to get into trouble here, and it might've been better if he hadn't chosen to act as his twin, but "I confess, I was curious what it would feel like. Being him. You were all so eager to meet me, get to know me. It felt nice."

"So you're a lonely old fool."

Carl winced. "Only a dozen years older than you—okay, I get your point. A fool."

Leo picked up his stick again and swatted at the grass tips.

"It made me and Mum so happy to think we met someone famous who enjoyed being around us."

Carl bowed his head.

A stick prodded into his arm. "I mean . . . I think I get why you thought it wouldn't matter. If your brother came and took over my lessons, then you've thought you've helped us. And I think I get why you kept pretending. It's mostly for me. To make me look good in front of those bullies."

"I really was trying to be good, wasn't I?" Carl preened.

Leo wagged a finger.

Fine, fine. Carl sank his head to his chest. "I guess I'll have to come clean with everyone."

Leo nodded. "You should do it while everyone's gathered together. Save having to admit your faults over and over."

Dread made Carl feel like he was made of stone and sinking into the earth. He didn't want to get up, but Leo's imploring look . . .

"I don't want to face the music," Carl admitted, heaving himself to his feet.

"You said we need to have courage to live our dreams."

"This isn't exactly my dream."

"You get the point."

Carl grumbled. "Fine. As long as you remember those words when it's your time to get up on stage."

Leo grimaced and tapped the end of his stick against his chin. "Deal."

"Excellent, now if you'd pull-slash-drag me back to the hall . . ."

Leo laughed, threw away his stick, and tugged Carl all the way there. Sage—in her wraparound dress—was making her way towards the volunteers seated around tables covered with cupcakes. Judging by her relieved smile, she'd come before the meeting had officially started.

Carl shuffled inside—aided by Leo at his back—as

Grayson finished answering some trivia question and jogged down the stairs from the stage. His gaze caught Carl's and swept across the hall to Sage, who was being praised by the teachers for her amazing cupcakes. "Uniform colours, that's a great idea. This'll add school spirit to the event."

The witches looked on with flattened lips, and one of them whispered loudly, "It's not like she gets much attention, she should store this in her memory."

Leo's hands stilled against his back.

Another witch murmured, "I can't believe her luck lately. What with Jason Lyall always hanging out with her."

"I'm sure it won't last."

Carl's chest sank as he took another step towards the stage—

Leo lunged and hugged him around the arm, dragging him backwards; Grayson shared a look with Leo and grabbed Carl's other arm, hauling him out of the main hall. The doors were shut behind them, and Leo and Grayson sagged, letting out a long breath towards Carl's sleeves.

Carl, his back pressed against the wall, eyed them both. "Wasn't I supposed to come clean?"

"Those mums are always embarrassing mine."

Grayson nodded grimly. "We'll think of a better way."

"Thank God," Carl said on a sigh. "Something's digging into my back."

Leo and Grayson let him go; he came off the wall and glanced at the framed photos he'd been resting against. They were pictures of teachers throughout the years, and school board volunteers. There were too many of those witches, and . . . that face looked familiar. From five years ago . . . Was that—

Before he could linger on the photo, a group of holiday program kids swarmed through the entrance and made for the kitchens, and he, Leo, and Grayson smuggled themselves smartly out of the stampede.

Outside, Grayson got a call, which he took begrudgingly and waved for Carl and Leo to head off to whatever they had planned next.

Leo was headed back to the bakery, and Carl needed to do the same. He fidgeted along the way, and once he was inside the quiet shop, met Poppy at the counter. The smile bestowed on Carl had him biting his lip. He could see it now Grayson wasn't around—those bright eyes following his every step, the hint of a leer in the quirk of his brow . . . all meant for him. No hidden history of a past fling that hadn't worked out and had never been forgotten. These looks were all for Carl. Well, for Jason. Fake Jason.

Still, it was empowering, and he could see why Grayson loved that sort of attention even if he never returned the feelings. Carl couldn't help but feel chuffed.

However, he wouldn't smile too much, lest Poppy get the wrong idea.

He cleared his throat and leaned against the counter. The lean angled too much towards intimate and he pushed himself back a step, jerking a thumb over his shoulder.

"Can we talk a minute?"

Poppy's smile grew hopeful. He tossed his apron to Leo and told him to man the counter. Four steps later, Poppy grabbed Carl's wrist and was hauling him outside—

Carl's foot caught on the darn threshold and he tripped, sending poor Poppy shooting down the stairs. Flailing, Carl readied himself to hit the footpath and possibly a passerby, but he was caught swiftly in Poppy's arms. And even twirled around with the momentum, Poppy all joyous laughter. "Falling right into my arms."

Carl caught a breath and glanced over Poppy's shoulder—

Two dozen feet away stood Grayson, frozen to the footpath, gaze rooted on them. There was something in his stance, shoulders slightly slumped, and his watchful gaze seemed to hold less depth than usual. Could that be the twitch of his jaw, or a trick of the light? Why did the usual charismatic aura around Grayson feel dulled? Greyed.

Something sharp shifted in Carl's chest and he quickly tried to extract himself from the hold, but Poppy held him tight and Grayson was ducking away into the café by the time he was finally free.

It must look like Carl had decided *for* the fling; even though Grayson shouldn't care about it, Carl felt nauseous. His heart galloped. He had a massive urge to *explain*.

Two pedestrians passed Carl and Poppy, heading into the bakery, and Poppy patted Carl's arm. "Better help Leo out. Can we save the talk for later?"

Except, Carl couldn't save it for later. It cribbled in his belly, rose up his throat, and burst out. "I don't want there to be a later."

Poppy stalled, frowning, and Carl tried again more calmly. "You seem like an interesting person, Poppy, but I don't fancy you."

He blinked and rubbed his jaw, glancing sidewards as he sighed. "It's Grayson, isn't it?"

Carl jumped. "Ha! No."

Poppy's eyebrow rose in disbelief.

Shaking his head harder, ignoring very loud, urgent *whispers*, Carl said, "It just . . . isn't you."

After a few beats, Poppy laughed lightly and shrugged. "I see. Worth a shot, I guess."

Carl kept glancing over the road, and Poppy shooed him on. "Off you go, then. I've got to help Leo in the shop."

Poppy retreated inside, and Carl clipped his way into the café, past patrons eating and answering trivia, and—where was Grayson?

"Looking for someone?" Carl turned towards the familiar voice. Linda, in the corner booth, eyeing him closely over a cream-filled raspberry lamington.

He shuffled over, still searching the café interior. "Have you seen Grayson?"

"He came, chugged down a glass of water, and left through the back."

Had Grayson's haste been to avoid him? Or had he wanted to give them space, and just happened to be thirsty?

Why was Carl thinking so hard on this?

It was like he *hoped* Grayson had hurried away in disappointment.

Stop being ridiculous.

Carl gnawed on his lip and plunked down on the seat opposite Linda. "What should I do?"

A question for the universe, really, but in her typical cryptic way, Linda answered. And her answer followed Carl around the rest of the day. "Ask yourself what makes a home. And you'll get there. You'll see."

“I haven’t the courage to keep tramping forever, without getting anywhere at all.”

L. Frank Baum

The Wonderful Wizard of Oz

Chapter Thirteen

W*hat makes a home. What makes a home . . .*

Carl spent the better part of the afternoon pacing his front porch, flicking through last month's magazine. Linda—with this emphasis on 'home'—must be a Taurus.

He slumped into the wicker chair, dropped the mag, and snatched a lavender frond tickling his ankles.

All this thought of 'home' had Carl knotted up inside. He'd run away from his. He'd convinced himself it was the best thing to do at the time, but . . . the truth was, he couldn't hide here forever.

He took out his phone and reread the message he'd received from Jason. 'Cousin' Cora might soon be engaged to her boyfriend, who had two girls.

The unsaid plea for him to admit the truth to Cora had him panicking, but the mention of those two girls . . . that punched hardest. He jammed his phone back into his pocket and tore at his lavender frond.

"What's that lavender ever done to you?"

At that curious voice, Carl swung his head around and leapt to his feet. Grayson came up the path, expression heavier than usual, with a bundle under his arm. For a flashing instant, that urge to explain today's moment on the footpath with Poppy returned—

And quickly dissipated. Carl didn't need to blurt all that out. It wasn't like there was anything between them. Besides, his chest was still too full of his mum.

Grayson's troubled gaze flickered to his and back to the shredded frond.

Carl ran his lavender scented fingers through his hair. "I was feeling . . . upset."

"*Was* feeling?" Grayson stepped onto the veranda, expression shifting into concern, and Carl . . . *liked* that Grayson was able to put aside whatever worries he had to ask about Carl's. It was kind and considerate and generous, and Carl's heart *absolutely did not* thump a few beats faster.

He slumped back into his seat and rested his head back, staring into the middle distance between them. "*Am* feeling."

Grayson dusted off an old stool and dragged it next to him. "Want to share?"

"You came here for a reason. Not this."

"Do I need a reason?" Grayson swallowed, glancing away. He shifted the bundle to his lap and Carl recognised Sage's wraparound dress—he'd left it at the school—along with the container from his burned soup.

Carl suddenly understood the bundle. It wasn't something to return, or something he'd left behind. It was an excuse so Grayson felt he could visit.

Carl's breath felt shallow and ticklish in his lungs. "Yes. You need a reason." Grayson frowned and Carl leaned forward in his chair, fishing for eye contact. "But the reason can be to see a friend."

After a moment, Grayson nodded slowly. "I wanted to see my friend. And now I want to know how you're feeling." He glanced at the leftover lavender. "Why are you upset?"

Carl sigh-groaned and flung himself dramatically back in his seat. "When I was chasing after you earlier I bumped into Linda, and she said I need to think about home."

Grayson straightened on his stool. "You chased . . ." He cleared his throat and kept the conversation on track. "Linda told you to think about home?"

"Yes, and it's been occupying my head the whole afternoon. Then my brother messaged me, and I'm still coming to terms with it."

Grayson waited patiently as Carl explained the mess he'd left behind. " . . . They're nice girls. I once cheered one of them up by tagging a lamppost. That got me a good fine but it stopped her tears. Still . . ." Carl grabbed at another lavender frond and Grayson saved it from decimation, placing a warm hand over his and pinching the frond free.

"Still, what?"

A long sigh. "If Cora gets married . . . she'll become a stepmum." His chin sank and his throat tightened. "The girls might even *call* her Mum, when *I've* never had the chance."

The stool skidded closer, and the block of Grayson's warmth hovered close. A comforting hand titled his chin, dragged to the crook of his neck and rested there. "You want to acknowledge her."

A nod.

"You want her to acknowledge you."

For the first time in Carl's life, the sting behind his eyes gave way to blurry vision and dampness down his cheek. Grayson had understood immediately. Said the words he'd not even admitted to himself. More than calling her Mum, he wanted her to call him her son. Hers. Someone worthy of a mother's unconditional love.

Grayson murmured, "It sounds like you have a close bond, even though you haven't shared the truth. Maybe it's her way of being there for you?"

"You-you think so?"

"She comes almost every day to hang with you at the store. That sounds like love to me."

Carl covered his face with his hands. "You always know what to say." He laughed croakily. "Something's not right about you. You're too perfect."

"Perfect?"

That sounded . . . Carl peeked between his fingers at the preening look Grayson had and snorted. "I spoke too soon."

Grayson returned to being serious. "I think, deep down, you want to talk with her."

Carl swallowed the lump in his throat and nodded.

"Want to practice?"

"Practice? How?"

Grayson considered this, eyed his bundle, took the wrap dress and flung it around his shoulders.

"Grayson!" Carl laughed, shoving him.

Grayson took it off again. "Practice facing her with me."

Carl took a deep breath and let it out slowly. "This feels weird."

"You can always be weird with me."

"That's weirdly reassuring."

"Imagine I'm your mother. I've come into your store and"—Grayson caught sight of the magazine Carl had abandoned earlier and plucked it up—"I'm about to read out your horoscope. Go."

Carl lowered the magazine Grayson was now flicking through. "I know the truth, Cora."

"Truth, what truth? Hahaha."

Carl winced. "*Without* putting on a female voice?"

Grayson cleared his throat and tried again.

"The truth about our relationship."

"You know?"

"I struggled to bring this up earlier. I didn't want to come across as ungrateful. Patricia did a lot of the heavy lifting growing up, and she is a 'mum' to me, but I've always had a bond with you too."

Grayson encouraged him to continue.

Carl hauled in a breath. "I know you are my birth parent. I know I have a twin brother. I also know you couldn't take care of both of us."

"Are you . . . angry?"

"No. I was hard enough for Patricia on my own. I don't fault you for adopting Jason out. Look where he got to because he was given a chance with a family who had the capacity to care for him."

Grayson had his hand now and was holding it tightly. Or perhaps Carl had grabbed his, and he was the one gripping hard.

"Still. It's shocking. And I felt lots of confusing things when I first met Jason. I have questions I've wanted to ask you and Patricia, and I've had to bear never getting answers. I didn't want to upset the status quo. Don't want to hurt Patricia's feelings, or make you uncomfortable. So, I keep running away from my feelings." Carl choked on his words, finding it difficult to continue. He really struggled with the idea of rocking the family boat. What if it distanced Patricia from him? What if Cora didn't want to be acknowledged and stopped her daily visits to avoid awkwardness? What if it cost him two people he cared about?

Carl looked at Grayson, panicking. "Do I really have to face this?"

Grayson gently squeezed his hand. "Perhaps confronting these feelings will be healing."

"Healing?"

A small, sympathetic smile. "Help to put your heart back together? Even one conversation can shift an entire perspective and jumpstart the heart. Maybe talking your feelings through, asking those questions, will help you feel more at ease with your family. Also with your ex."

"How can you be so sure things can change in as little as one conversation?"

Grayson's eyes beheld Carl, dark, intense, happy, frustrated. "I know."

Carl doubled his grip on Grayson's poor hand. He opened his mouth to speak and was cut off by the shrill ring of Grayson's phone.

Grayson disentangled their hands and answered. "Mr Wilson. Yes, I'm coming this evening. I'll grab a bite to eat and be right there." He finished the call and looked regretfully at Carl.

Carl nodded and stood. He meant to say *that's okay, no problem, chat later*. But . . .

He took the bundle off Grayson's lap, set it on his wicker chair and jerked a thumb towards the gate. "Can I be your PA tonight?"

JASON CALLED WHILE THEY WERE ORDERING DINNER. AFTER HIS twin's last message, Carl wasn't sure he wanted to answer, but Grayson gave him the courage.

He glanced around the busy eatery, caught sight of one of the witches in the line behind him, and answered the call. "Jason here."

"Just wondering," the true Jason said slowly.

"Wondering?"

"Who exactly is Angus?"

Momentary relief. Just curiosity about Angus.

Carl stiffened. If Jason was asking about the mechanical bull they liked to ride, usually on birthdays or—

This must have to do with Pete's stag night.

He waited for the hit of hurt. There was a slight heave in his chest, but . . . not as painful as he'd thought. A slow breath trickled out of him. He looked at Grayson, whose back was to Carl as he scanned the menu and glanced back for Carl's order. The little question, the consideration to order together—it had gravity racing through him again—

Grayson raised a brow.

Carl caught himself, mouthed he'd have the same, finished off his call—

And slapped his cheeks with both hands. *What outrageous things are you thinking?*

While munching on their food at an outdoor table, Grayson said, "Don't take me paying for you the wrong way."

Carl's fork hovered mid-air, a few inches from his mouth. The wrong way. Was he referring to how the lawyers had paid for lunch and made him feel inferior?

Or was he making sure Carl didn't think this was in any way romantic?

Carl scoffed down his mouthful of potato gratin and chased it with water. He hedged his answer so it covered both options. "Friends can take turns paying without it getting weird. I'll get it next time."

Almost like déjà vu, Carl followed Grayson to his gig working for the former Air Force pilot, and Mr Wilson escorted them through the house and the back garden to the standalone unit.

"Wifi's down," Mr Wilson said. "I hope you can manage without?"

"Better that way," Grayson said. "No distractions."

Mr Wilson's gaze drifted to Carl. "Is that right?" He waved at them and left them to their laptop devices—and the dodgy door.

Grayson propped the door open with one of the many file

boxes on the bed, and at a rush of southerly wind, exchanged it with just the lid of a box.

The two of them alone in the small unit had Carl strangely clammy. He hurriedly got his laptop up and running.

"You don't have to actually work," Grayson said. "You're welcome to hang next to me."

Carl wagged a finger. "You wait. I'll have more done than you by the end of the evening."

Grayson chuckled, but his chuckle did not last long. Not when he saw Carl's new method: speaking into the microphone and having all the words magically appear on his screen.

At Grayson's surprise, Carl said, "Sage showed me this."

"Clever."

Carl agreed, and they dove into transcribing for another hour, until they felt the need for a hot drink to combat the draught coming through the cracked-open door.

"Any food?" Grayson asked as he finished typing up a page.

Carl peered into the cupboards. "Lots of tea. A dodgy looking tin of diced tomatoes. And some multi-vitamins."

"Throw me a couple of multi-vitamins. I don't want to catch another cold."

Carl handed over a steaming tea and two tablets, and took a couple himself. "You might also want to tone down how much you work if you don't want to get sick all the time."

Grayson sipped his tea, humming noncommittally.

"You don't have to . . ." Carl stopped. Guilt harnessed Grayson like a horse—made him work, made him *sick*. And Carl wished he'd stop. Give himself time to heal.

"Don't have to what?"

"Work so hard."

Grayson's nose stayed dipped into his cup for a long time. He set the cup down and drew a finger around the steam-moistened rim. "Perhaps I should tone it down."

Carl held a hopeful breath and nodded.

"Especially if I have other priorities."

"Other priorities?"

"Spending time with people I care about. For leisure."

Carl was still holding his breath. "Like whom?"

Grayson circled his nail around the cup again.

"*Sam*?"

The cup toppled and Grayson quickly caught it. "Where did *that* come from?"

"Spending time. Priorities . . . I just . . ." Carl threw up his hands. "I wondered."

Grayson stared at him with a flicker of something like curiosity. Or hope, or disbelief, or caution—or perhaps *all* of that in rapid succession. When he spoke again, he spoke quietly, carefully, and his gaze didn't once waver from Carl's, which made Carl feel restless.

"Sam is my past. A part of my journey. Not my destination."

"If you were both in love you might—"

"No."

Simply said. Just that. And Carl sank back into his chair, nodding and nodding.

Grayson opened his mouth to add something and shut it. Then said, "As for work . . . I should probably consider doing less, but I do like odd jobs. Helping others, variation."

"You prefer that over a career? Moving up the ladder?"

"Yes."

There was something extremely comforting in this conviction, and Carl rubbed his damp hands over his nape, nodding again.

"I'm privileged, of course. I have a mortgage-free house, and an inheritance. I can afford to pick and choose."

"You know, your ability to do . . . everything, would be a real asset in a small town."

Dark eyes lifted to his. "A small town like yours?"

Carl pushed him lightly away, trying to ignore the winding feeling in his chest.

Grayson cleared his throat. "You said you work in a convenience store. Like a dairy."

"Bit bigger than the ones here, but yeah."

"What's it like?"

Carl brightened. He could feel his spirits lift and his voice became animated as he told Grayson about some of his Convenience Store (mis)Adventures.

"Working there gives you joy," Grayson said.

"It's not particularly glamorous."

"Does glamour equal joy?"

Carl hesitated. "The attention Jason gets for his accomplishments is nice."

"You've got the locals coming in to gossip. Is that not fun attention too? Is that not nice?"

Carl stared at Grayson. And stared. There was a shift in his chest, and an abrupt wistful longing for his store. All this . . . from a conversation with Grayson. "You don't think it's a dead end? Lacks integrity?"

"I think it sounds full of character. I'd like to see it—you, working there."

Butterflies slammed into his chest. He managed a nonchalant shrug. "Come and stay anytime."

A gust of wind had the door flying open and the box lid flying free into the room. Grayson twisted his chair and lunged, but the door moved too fast, hitting the frame of the bed, bouncing back—and slamming shut.

Grayson yanked at the handle, jiggling it. It didn't open.

Carl was on his feet, shifting nervously, as he handed Grayson his phone.

Grayson called Mr Wilson's number. Carl could hear it ringing at their end—could see light and movement from the house—but Mr Wilson wasn't picking up.

"On silent?" Carl speculated.

"Or his TV is too loud."

"Try again."

"Can we use your phone?"

"I followed you on a whim. You brought all the electronics. Mine's at the villa."

"You don't always have your phone on you?"

"Half the time. This isn't that half."

Grayson pressed the button on his phone but the screen wasn't flashing any colours.

"Yours *died*?"

"We're stuck in a cabin with no wifi and only one bed. Of course my phone died."

Carl snickered. "Of course."

They looked at one another and, simultaneously, with great urgency, banged on the door, shouting.

The gusty winds did them no favours. Their voices were lost. The universe was laughing.

They eyed one another, and shot their gazes elsewhere.

Away from the king-single bed!

Carl ran a hand through his hair and pointed to their laptops. "I suppose we'll pull an all-nighter."

"Right. Yes."

They buried themselves diligently in Mr Wilson's words, one speaking hurriedly into the laptop, and the other typing furiously.

From time to time, Carl snuck a peek at Grayson; from time to time, Carl felt the prickle along his profile as Grayson snuck a peek at him.

Close to midnight, and twenty thousand words—and an awkward moment in which they had to take turns relieving themselves using an old Coke bottle—they snuck looks at the same time.

Grayson pushed his chair back from the desk. "Okay. Let's address the flying monkey in the room."

Carl's gaze flew from the bed to the Coke bottle to the bed again. "You mean the crowd of them? Each with a pair of immense and powerful wings?"

"Chattering with a great deal of noise."

Carl snickered and turned his chair to face Grayson squarely. "We don't need to be this coy. We're friends. We can . . . And we can share a bed."

Grayson hesitated. A glimmer of a frown touched his brow, and then he inclined his head sharply. "Exactly."

They averted their gaze.

The air felt thick when it came time to shimmy out of their jeans. They turned their backs to one another and hurriedly shoved them off, but the *flump* of material hitting the ground sounded extra loud to Carl's ears.

Grayson hit the lights, and Carl blessed the dark as he climbed under the cool sheets. He kept as close to the wall as he could, practically in the gap between bed and wall, and still it wasn't enough distance to thin the tension between them.

Every movement Grayson made puffed the blankets and air scuttled over Carl until he was thrumming with shivers. Shivers that didn't dissipate, even though the heat of Grayson's body radiated over him.

Carl stared into the dark, acutely aware of his breathing, of Grayson's. It sounded so loud in the quiet of the room. He shifted from his back to his side, facing the shadowy form beside him. He wanted to say something, act normal, break the tautness in the air.

Grayson must have had a similar thought. He shifted onto his side too and his rumbly voice vibrated over the pillow.

"If this will be a problem to explain to Poppy—"

Carl's heart galloped, and his mouth dried. He told himself

to swallow it back, but couldn't. "Why would it be a problem? I told Poppy I'm not interested in him."

The sound of a swallow. "You're not?"

Nervousness jolted through him, a multitude of electrical spikes. He couldn't handle it. He whipped himself onto his other side, back to Grayson, facing the wall, and slammed his eyes shut. "I'm not. Good night." He feigned a yawn, and then sleep.

A long moment passed, and Grayson's sigh stirred at the back of his head. "That's . . . Night, Carl."

"Dear me," said the Voice, "how sudden! Well, come to me tomorrow, for I must have time to think it over."

L. Frank Baum

The Wonderful Wizard of Oz

Chapter Fourteen

After many hours playing possum, hoping Grayson couldn't hear his wildly beating heart, Carl eventually drifted to sleep. And a deep one at that. It had to have been, because Carl was waking up to the feeling of warmth at his chest, around his waist, under his curled leg.

He slit his eyes open, gulped quietly, and shut them again. He was tangled around Grayson, half on top of the man like a snug blanket.

He daren't move. Daren't *breathe*. Or he'd . . . rub against Grayson's hip, and Grayson would rub against his inner thigh.

This wouldn't do.

He should extract himself. Somehow.

He whimpered and prayed Grayson would keep sleeping. His breathing seemed steady and even, lips parted like he was deep in a dream.

Every muscle tensed as Carl carefully lifted his arm off Grayson's stomach, and then his leg from those warm hips . . . He held his breath and painstakingly shifted inch by inch away until he was crawling to the end of the bed, where he slid on his jeans and indulged in burying his face in his hands and shaking his head.

Oh *God*. He knew what this was. Knew what was happening here. He kept trying to talk himself out of it, but the effort was futile . . .

He was . . . he was . . .

"What are you fretting about?" Grayson's voice behind him had Carl leaping to his feet, squealing.

Grayson swung his legs out of bed, long glorious, toned legs, and—

Carl threw up his arms and paced the room. "There's no slapping myself silly anymore. I'm screwed. I can't believe I'm . . ."

"You're what?"

He wagged a finger at Grayson, because really, this was All. His. Fault. "I'm your groupie!"

Grayson grabbed Carl's finger and moved it down, lips twitching. "We've *long* established that."

Carl's finger shot back up, warningly, and Grayson held his hands up in surrender. "For real this time. Somewhere along the line, somewhere in one of our conversations, I started looking at you with hearts in my eyes. Big sparkly ones!"

Grayson stepped forward to take hold of Carl's arms, probably to give his heartbreaker speech, and Carl was not in the mood. Enough to realise he'd fallen so far for Grayson that he might risk handing over his heart again. Not just hand it over, either. There was an overwhelming, terrifying compulsion to *throw* it to him. To declare this heart was his. Handle as you like!

Insanity.

Carl shook his head. But his body—wow, it was still abuzz.

"Oh my *God*, I'm burning for you."

When Grayson opened his lips, Carl slapped a hand over any words about to emerge. "Nope. Uh uh."

Like a gift from the heavens, the door swung open and Mr Wilson popped his head in. "You two should've called me. I'd have let you out last night."

Carl was an impolite stare, and he wagged his finger at ancient Mr Wilson too. "Also your fault."

With that, he skirted out the door, and ran away with the wind.

~

THE IDEA WAS TO SPEND THE DAY AVOIDING GRAYSON AND indulging in panic. But Grayson made it particularly difficult. Every other corner, those dark eyes confronted him.

The first time, at Houghton Bay. Carl had biked there furiously, thinking an icy dip in the sea would help cool him off. No sooner had he taken off his trusty Toto when a vehicle came to a halt on the curb beside him. Recognising the ute, Carl startled, jammed his helmet back on, and—after shaking his head at the dark-haired heartbreaker behind the wheel—took off once more.

The second time, at Sage's place. He'd gone after Leo texted asking for his help with the talent show. Carl reminded him he couldn't locate the C key on the piano and Leo said Carl was there to help decide on a costume. Halfway through this costume design project, who should knock on the door pretending to drop off Leo's favourite apple cake?

Grayson extended the cake towards a grinning Leo while his gaze set over his shoulder on Carl and his gaping mouth. "Like the costume, kiddo."

"I wanted to wear another one, but Carl said it reminded him of a frightening picture he once saw."

Grayson's brows shot up, and Carl laugh-cried as he slunk out the back door and made a dashing roly-poly leap over the fence.

The third time those gently judgy eyes confronted him was an hour later, at the outcrop overlooking Wellington. Carl had collapsed onto the bench and tipped his head into the afternoon sun.

A shadow passed over his face; he opened his eyes and found Grayson's gaze boring into him from above.

"Gah! You meerkat. Popping up everywhere."

An upside-down smirk. "I think you want me to find you. Or . . ."

"Or?"

Grayson bowed over him and as their noses touched, he veered to Carl's ear, leaving a wake of shivers over his cheek. "You wouldn't be retracing our meet-cutes."

Carl hauled in a deep breath to deny this, but . . . he really had ended up at their first three meet-cutes. The Beach, where Grayson had rescued his bike. The Street Greet, where Carl had finally learned his name. The Cliff, where they'd first fallen atop one another. "Dammit."

Grayson came around the bench, laughing, and sat beside Carl. A warm presence, snug. Nerve wrecking.

They stared at the green vista of Wellington with shimmery seas in the distance, and Carl gulped. "Are you here to do your heartbreaker thing?"

"Tsk. I ate your soup, remember?"

"What does that mean?"

"It means, even if it tastes awful, I'll eat it so you never feel bad."

"You don't want me to feel bad." Carl narrowed his gaze at Grayson. "You're going to break my heart in a way I'm happy about?"

Grayson tsked again.

Lightning bolted down Carl's middle. "You mean . . . you *like* me?"

"I do."

Carl blinked hard—and shuffled right up against Grayson, nose practically in his cheek. "You find me attractive?"

Grayson tipped his head up and reluctantly sighed. "Yes."

"As in, *you want to sleep with me*?"

"I want that, too."

"What is going on here? My heart is trying to jump out of my chest."

"Mine feels the same."

"I thought yours was broken."

"You jumpstarted it."

Carl leapt off the bench and paced the outcrop back and forth. "Explain."

"Sit down. I'm afraid you'll tumble over the edge."

Carl plunked his baffled bum back on the bench.

Grayson scrubbed his face. "It happened. Suddenly. You opened my mind up about my mother wanting me to find happiness. You encouraged me to like again, without the guilt." He shook his head with a grimace. "You made those incredulous moaning sounds getting your toes done . . ."

Happened. Suddenly. Toes—"Is *that* why you raced off to the bus stop?"

Grayson gave him a stern look. "It was the anniversary of my mother's passing and I was . . ." He glanced towards his lap.

"Good call." A pause. "You suddenly liked me?"

"I tried ignoring it."

"That's why you didn't answer my texts for help with Leo's lesson."

"I wanted to shake off these . . . feelings, but when I overheard Poppy was going to be at Sage's dinner, that it was supposed to be some kind of blind date . . ." Grayson balled his fists. "I tried telling myself not to care, to leave it be."

But he couldn't. "You came to the dinner instead."

"The *thought* of you with Poppy . . ." Grayson's glare was something. So epic, Carl fucking fluttered.

"You really were the jealous suitor. I told you—I turned him down."

"I don't know how I slept at all last night. Things kept . . . shifting, in my chest." His Adam's apple bulged with a swallow, and dark eyes turned to Carl. His voice grew gruff. "You mumbled for me to stop tossing and turning, locked your leg around me, and flung an arm across my middle. Everything wound tight inside. So tight. I could barely breathe."

"Sounds like you're a lost cause."

"What'll you do about it, groupie?"

"I don't know." A hoppy laugh escaped Carl seeing Grayson struggle to maintain a scowl. "Get it out of our system?"

"We could try." A pause. "But I'm afraid—"

"Afraid what?"

Grayson swallowed and leapt to his feet. "Ah, I'm afraid we can't try that *right* now. We're due to help Sage at an escape room in twenty minutes."

"We are?"

"Leo was upset you bolted before he could ask you along."

Grayson strode towards the path. Carl followed him down the hill to his ute; the air felt taut between them, every shared look came with an electric shiver, and Carl decided it would be best to change the subject. Talk about things that didn't make his chest go haywire. Like Sage and Leo, and how Carl ought to tell Sage the truth. How she might take it. And whether Carl *really* had to tell her. And—"I'd rather talk about me liking you," he muttered.

Grayson laughed and ruffled his hair, and Carl liked it so much, he imagined cartoon hearts popping up all around him.

He shook his head and folded his arms in self-disgrace.

"We should stop oscillating between scowling and smiling," Grayson said.

"You seem to be smiling more than scowling." But then, he'd had longer to come to terms with this.

Grayson's gaze flickered out the window. "Here we are."

Carl couldn't jump out of the ute fast enough, and he was in the lobby in under thirty seconds.

His step stalled as he took in the room, bustling with energy and eager participants. The witches were looming over the reception desk and came away from it with tickets in hand and pointy chins tipped up in cackling laughter. Sage and Leo were tucked into a corner, beside large vintage posters and a shelf of curious brain teasing logic artifacts. Two doors came off the lobby at either end—to the left, a whimsical rainbow promised a journey to Oz; to the right, where the witches had gathered, was the obviously more popular Haunted House.

Carl had taken a look online in the ute—this Haunted escape room was a city favourite.

Grayson caught up to him and took in the volunteer team-building group; in sync, they beelined to Sage and Leo.

Before they got there, the witches—all wearing matching green scarves—slunk over. "Here are your tickets. The Haunted House is at maximum capacity so you guys will have to do the kid room."

Another witch piped in, "It fits you. Your bakery has an Oz theme. Over the Raindough." She patted Sage's shoulder in a way that had Carl gritting his teeth. "Should be easier, too."

An escape room worker in a red uniform sidled over with a wide smile. "Just because the Oz room is more colourful, doesn't mean it's lacking in depth." To Sage, she said, "Better for sure."

Carl liked this worker immediately. So did Leo, judging by his awed look at her.

The witches huffed quietly. "Shall we make a race of it?

Your team and ours? We win, you give us free coffee for a month. You win, we come in and buy coffee every day for a month."

Sage held her head high and smiled brightly. "Looking forward to having you as regular customers."

The witches turned on their heels, heading for the Haunted House door. As soon as their backs turned, Sage sagged. She glanced over at Carl and Grayson, terrified.

Carl understood. He was nervous too. This was far too close to Quiz Night for his liking, but by golly, he'd do his best to beat those witches. He slicked on a confident smile and gave her a thumbs up, then leaned to Grayson and murmured, "You know how you taught me being smart wasn't attractive?"

"I recall."

"Could you be *not attractive* right now? For the next hour?"

"I'll be downright hideous."

"This is why I like you."

Grayson bought tickets for himself and Carl, and they hooked arms with Leo and Sage and followed a painted-on yellow brick road to The Emerald Escape.

The first room was all black and white, and dimly lit. Several boxes sat randomly on the floor. Mist pumped into the room, thickening the air, and speakers pumped out anxious music and wind sounds. Projected onto the ceiling was a large twister.

"Spooky. What do we do?" Leo asked.

Sage murmured, "Hope most of this is like spot the difference. Something that doesn't require much brains."

"But we *have* brains," Carl said, trying to sound upbeat. "We can decipher stuff. What's that thingy?"

Leo and Sage sighed. "We are so screwed."

"Screwed on!" Grayson said with far too much enthusiasm.

"Screwed up," Carl amended.

A hand landed on his head and rubbed fondly.

Sage jumped with renewed vigour. "Gray, you can do the hard stuff, and look, Jason. A piano. Something for you."

Carl whimpered.

"Actually," Leo said, leaping to his rescue, "can I try cracking that one? I think we have to find the sheet music and play the right keys in the right order. You'd let me practice, wouldn't you, Jason?"

Carl straightened. "Of course. The experienced should always give way for the developing. Playing under pressure will help improve your skills vastly. As they say, practice makes perfect—" At looks from Leo and Grayson, Carl choked on his inane platitudes and cleared his throat. "Carry on."

Leo scurried ahead, calling out for the rest of them to look for musical notes. They were found under, over, and in nick-nacks around the room, and once Leo had lined them up in order, he played.

With a click, the wall beside the piano opened, and the four of them crawled through a long and narrow tunnel to—

Brightness.

The next room was all colours of the rainbow. Welcome to Oz.

They gathered in the middle of the yellow brick road. It stretched across the room and disappeared into a wall mural leading to the Emerald City. Four life-size figures were planted around the room. Sage raised her hand. "I get this. The tinman and the lion and the scarecrow and Dorothy—they're in the wrong places."

They each took a figure and planted it on its correct base and waited . . .

Nothing happened.

Carl double checked. Dorothy first, the scarecrow who wants brains, the tinman who wants a heart, the lion who wants to be courageous. Wait, was that a smaller base beside Dorothy?

"Ohh, ohh, I got it. We're missing Toto."

"I don't see a dog anywhere," Sage said.

"I know, I know." Leo tugged his mum's sleeve. "I saw Toto in the first room. Help me get it. He was in one of the big boxes."

Two heads of straw-coloured hair ducked and disappeared into the tunnel to the first room, leaving behind Carl and Grayson and a truck-load of tension.

Grayson edged over to the tinman and fidgeted with his clock-heart, trying to straighten it to some invisibly perfect line.

Carl shouldn't find the nervous tic quite this charming. But he did. Before he knew it, he was slinking up behind Grayson, observing how his ears reddened.

Carl touched the tip of his finger to the shell of one. "How did you get that scar?"

Goosebumps lifted on the back of Grayson's neck; he clamped a palm over his nape. "Surfing. Clipped a rock."

"Pity you can't wear a helmet. Have your own trusty Toto."

Grayson glanced at him, and took in the themed walls around them. "You seriously named my helmet Toto?"

"Those first days here, I felt pretty far away from home."

"And now?" Grayson sounded like he was suppressing his curiosity. He even sucked in his lips as if to keep from prying more.

"Well, Wellington is so green, it could be the Emerald City."

Grayson turned to face Carl fully. "Does that mean you're closer to home?"

Carl swallowed.

A grey glimmer hit Grayson's eye but he quickly smiled. "I might have some silver tap shoes somewhere, if you want to click your heels—"

Carl elbowed him, chuckling. But it wasn't a chuckle of humour. It felt heavy. "Stop."

Grayson looked away from him, and his voice thickened. "You need to have your conversations." He adjusted the tinman's heart again.

"Not today." Carl leaned in and turned Grayson's chin until he faced him. "Today we have to deal with feelings."

Ka-thunk, ka-thunk, ka-crazy-thunk.

Carl croaked, "Didn't you promise?"

The half inch separating them disappeared. Warm lips pressed softly against Carl's, and Carl took a sharp intake of air. Electricity sparked. Crackled.

Carl closed his eyes and felt Grayson's soft breath trickle into his mouth and spill over his bottom lip. "Gosh," he murmured, "it might take a fair bit to get this out of my system."

A sudden smile formed around Carl's unintentional one, followed by a naughty slip of tongue . . .

Carl hiccupped, and laughed. He pressed his lips—

Leo and Sage crawled back into the room and within the second, they'd ripped themselves apart, Carl spinning to face the wall where he spent a good ten seconds fanning his face.

"Got the dog!"

As soon as the figurine was set in place there came a series of clicks and a drawer popped out of a wall. A map, of the Emerald City. Clues hidden around the room helped them match landmarks to points on the map, and the area where everything intercepted revealed another riddle. Together, they answered the Wicked Witch's Stumper, unlocked the next door to The Courageous Path, translated the Flying Monkey Cipher, found a pivotal clue in a miniature Poppy Field; found the Witch's Broomstick, and unlocked a large closet filled with emerald green light.

The light waned, revealing a large mirror at the back and magnetised alphabet letters scattered on the wooden floor.

"Heartfelt Reflection," Grayson read. "What's the most important thing in the world?"

"Home," Leo called. "What Dorothy wants most."

"Not so sure," Carl said. "She wants to go home to the people that love her. It's love that's most important."

"But scarecrow, lion, and tinman all end up loving her, if it was about love, wouldn't she stay?"

Grayson was still staring into the mirror, unmoving, and there was something about his gaze that had Carl shifting from foot to foot. "She might have found a new family on her adventures, and she might even love them back, but . . ."

Grayson snapped out, "But there's no place like home."

Sage tucked Leo under her arm. "If you find someone you love very much one day, I hope you'll also return."

"Listen to your mum," Grayson said gruffly. "If she ever asks you home, go right away."

Carl's throat tightened. He touched Grayson's sleeve quietly and dark eyes lifted to his, a struggle in their depths. "Home is most important."

He said it like he was reminding himself. Reminding Carl: he must go home too. He must not make the same mistake Grayson did.

Carl felt the swell of emotion and the need to calm it. He lifted onto his toes and whispered in Grayson's ear, "Remember what she'd most want for you."

Grayson let out a shuddered breath over his cheek. Carl made sure to look into those dark eyes until he was sure Grayson had understood. Then he rocked back on his heels, picked through the magnets, and wrote the four-letter answer on the mirror.

LOVE.

The mirror swung open, and there was the lobby.

They'd done it.

They were one step from freedom.

"We must cross this strange place in order to get to the other side."

L. Frank Baum

The Wonderful Wizard of Oz

Chapter Fifteen

To say Sage was elated they'd finished before the witches . . . would be an understatement. She was so thrilled she invited Carl and Grayson to a celebratory dinner.

"They'll be drowning in coffee!"

Her good mood was infectious, and soon they were all laughing over tiramisu and Grayson's knees were knocking against Carl's under the table. Each knock sent a small spark through his middle; at one point, it was so strong he held his breath. Something Grayson seemed to notice—he slipped his hand over Carl's knee and gave him a reassuring squeeze.

Carl glanced at him. Glared.

Grayson barely swallowed a cocky smirk.

When dinner was over and they returned to the ute, Carl rubbed clammy palms over his still-tingling knees and side-eyed Grayson.

He was feeling particularly shivery and a whole lot of his body wanted more of those sparks, but there was a bit of brain flashing a warning sign. Grayson had become a friend, someone Carl loved talking to, going to the beach with, enjoying bike rides together. Could he keep that—even if long-distance—if they let this spiral out of control?

On the other hand, getting it out of their systems could be considered . . . mutual healing. They'd both been nursing hurt hearts for far too long. This infatuation with one another might be a step towards moving on, and who better to share this part of the journey with than someone they trusted?

A soft rumble hit Carl's ear. "Why're you biting your lip like that?"

Carl jumped in his seat. Red from the traffic light beamed over Grayson's face, those dark eyes trained on Carl's lips . . .

He swallowed and Grayson swept his gaze upwards. The air *crackled*. Nerves shot from his stomach to the base of his throat, and his voice came out gravelly. "Let's deal with these feelings."

"Yes." He said it simply and easily, and Carl's heart thundered.

"At your house?"

"Where there'll only be Carl."

Those words were butterflies in his belly; they made him restless and itchy.

Since they'd woken in a tangle of limbs, this feeling had been growing—and wildly out of control, at that. Every other shared look between them held curiosity and little zings of *awareness*. And after that kiss . . .

His whole body craved connection.

Grayson parked outside his house, on a not-particularly-dignified angle, and turned off the engine. In seconds he was out of the ute, coming around and opening Carl's door. Carl climbed out, breath hitching as Grayson cuffed a hand around his wrist and pulled him aside as he shut the door. Carl laughed nervously. "Why're you helping me out of the truck?"

Grayson's dark gaze hooked Carl deeply, his voice also rumbling with nerves. "Perhaps I'm afraid you'll run away?"

Carl took Grayson's wrist and pulled him until he folded forward. He brushed their lips together, a lingering, ticklish touch under a darkened sky. "Take me home."

~

"I THINK WE SHOULD DO THIS WITH THE LIGHTS ON."

"To better see me," Grayson agreed, eliciting a light whack from Carl.

"No, I just can't do it under a creepy puppeteer."

A tut. "You and this picture."

Carl laughed, and they fell onto the bed in a limb-tangling embrace. He kissed the smirk quirking Grayson's lips and outlined his nose with the tip of a blunt finger. The room was cool from having a window cracked open an inch, and the fresh scent of nature seeped into the room. The moment they'd stepped inside Grayson's house, they'd been a flurry of movement down the hall, stripping off shoes and jackets and pants and all their outer layers. And now Grayson lay under him in soft boxers and a shirt so thin it might not be defined as a shirt at all. Carl could see everything through it.

He swallowed a satisfied smile and wrapped himself tighter around Grayson's heady warmth. His thighs practically burned against Carl's. Even where their toes pressed—and fought—was warm. Nothing, of course, was hotter than Grayson's black gaze boring into him.

Last night, he'd noticed this feeling. Carl had wondered how much had been in his head. But he wasn't imagining this, the mutual sparks. And tonight, they were burning brighter.

Carl inhaled the cooler breath of nature and then burrowed his face into the crook of Grayson's neck to breathe in the thick taste of musk and salt. Ridiculous, how good he smelled. Even more ridiculous how easy it felt, rubbing himself all over Grayson. Like . . . like they'd never not done this. Both extremely comfortable, and extremely exciting. Honestly, his heart was tripping on itself just with this.

Healing, absolutely.

They battled with their bright magenta toes, the slight shifts a pleasant pressure where their lengths rubbed.

Hot fingers slid between Carl's and squeezed.

Grayson rumbled his name at the shell of his ear and it sent a sharp thrill through him.

"Again."

"You're incredible, Carl."

He parted Carl's legs with his knee, tightened their fingers, and in a breathless second the room tipped and Carl's back hit the mattress. Delicious weight descended on him, and more murmurs of his name mushed against his lips as they kissed.

Carl had been prepared for hot and heavy, perhaps with a good dose of awkward, but he'd never thought such a moment, such a first, could be so intense and intimate and wondrously addictive . . .

Their kisses deepened, slickened. Their breaths became pants, and still Grayson found moments to pepper in his name. *Carl. Carl. Carl.*

Grayson insisted with passion that Carl know Grayson knew who he was with. Each time he uttered his name, it came with a chase of gravity. Carl could barely catch his breath. He was being seen, admired, wanted, desired. His heart grew and pounded, and he wanted so much to share this immeasurable gift. To give back. Give something so Grayson's heart would release all the guilt and responsibility it held. Would gallop so fast he'd never be able to rein it in again. Would feel whole again.

Carl untangled one hand, slipped it up the back of Grayson's neck and threaded his fingers through his hair. He pulled Grayson back an inch and looked into those dark eyes that had never stopped *seeing* Carl. His breath hitched. "You're beautiful."

Grayson's lips twitched cheekily; Carl lifted his head, quickly kissing his "I know" away. He dragged his fingers from Grayson's head, over his shoulder, to his chest. "I mean here too."

Grayson dipped his mouth and captured Carl's in a fierce kiss. He dragged his lips and teeth along Carl's jaw and bit down lightly on his neck. "I want more of you."

Carl tugged at Grayson's t-shirt and helped peel it off him. His own came off next. Their naked chests met and Carl gasped. "Have all of me."

Grayson shut his eyes and swallowed thickly. "I hope you mean it."

Of course, Carl did. He kissed him, and kissed him again. Grayson could feast on him any way he pleased. "Start already. Want to feel you for a long time."

Grayson steered a large hand under Carl's boxers, pulling them down over his hip. The fabric teased over his sensitive skin and Carl *ached*. Off too came the last scrap of material covering Grayson, and Carl caught his breath in a horrified chuckle. "You're not real. How are you perfect everywhere?"

Grayson started to preen and Carl snatched his face into a punishing kiss. "I should never have fed your ego."

They laughed softly, each puff against Carl's face a caress. Quiet. Gentle.

His heart had already been pounding, but with this, each pound echoed shivers throughout his entire body. More shivers raced over him at the touch of a small breeze when Grayson briefly pulled away to rummage in his side drawer.

Grayson lowered himself, all that warmth and muscle, onto Carl.

Carl breathed deeply, chest expanding against Grayson's,

and slid his hands around firm hips, drawing him flush. "Say it again."

"Carl."

The rub of their hardened lengths had Carl's balls tightening. He shifted a leg and locked it around the back of Grayson's, canting his hips. "I'm yours."

Kisses suctioned onto Carl's throat as Grayson rocked against him and Carl made indecipherable sounds.

"You're even louder than you were getting our toes done."

Carl snatched a kiss. "I'm not shy about pleasure."

"I recall you blurting out you're into PDA."

"I wasn't trying to seduce you. I was on the phone!"

"Sure. If you say so."

Carl whacked him lightly on the back of the head and fell into another moan at Grayson's wicked swivel. He raised his head and snogged Grayson deeply. "You are so annoying."

Grayson laughed, the twinkle in his eye turning devilish, and suddenly cool wet fingers were dipping inside him.

A groan rumbled through the both of them, vibrating against their clashing lips. Grayson cuffed Carl's length, more lube coating him. Each stroke exploded in goosebumps and had him grabbing at Grayson's arms, shoulders, hair . . .

It'd been so long since he'd had this . . . Had he ever actually had this? Sex that felt so easy and natural, and so bloody intense . . .

He needed . . . needed . . .

Grayson understood. Read Carl like an open magazine. He rolled on a condom and bundled Carl up.

Dark eyes fused onto his as Grayson nudged inside him. Nerves leapt to life in brilliant bolts. He felt it race to his nipples, the end of his nose, his pinkie fingers.

More.

Carl trembled and mumbled incoherently, something about *coming home faster—*

Grayson pushed into him, stretching and stretching. He felt Grayson's pulse, the shivers that rattled him, the heavy gasp against his jaw when he'd fully seated himself. He rocked and groaned, and there was a quality to the groan that had Carl's heart skipping a beat. "*Live here forever.*"

Carl cupped his face, pulled him close, and brushed a sigh along his lips.

Grayson moved in and out of him in a perfectly lazy rhythm that quickly had Carl on the brink and screwing up handfuls of the sheets. He flexed around Grayson and uttered a whine.

Grayson drew all the way out and surged back inside him. "*Hear you, Carl.*"

He thrust with mounting speed and passion and Carl had never felt so understood and taken care of. Grayson's sweat-slickened abs rubbing against him was deliciously unbearable. "Gray . . ."

The shortened name moaned into his ear had Grayson pinning Carl's hands to the mattress. He threaded their fingers together and plunged into him, and—

Too much. Too good.

Every inch of his body came alive with sensation, from his fingers and toes to his ears and the backs of his knees.

Carl unravelled.

Grayson did too, their gasps mingling as he pushed deep inside a final time. Pulsing and spilling, Carl wrapped his arms around Grayson, clinging to him. And when finally, finally the waves ebbed, Carl closed his eyes against a firm shoulder.

That was . . . intense.

Grayson's weight sank atop him for a few moments before he pushed up on his elbows. "How're you doing?"

"You mean, do I have you out of my system yet?"

A shadow passed over Grayson's face. He quietly pulled out

and turned his back as he dealt with things. "Let me grab you a cloth."

But Carl was already swinging off the bed. His body—and his mind—were thrumming and it was too much. "I've got it."

He grabbed his clothes and dashed to the bathroom, where he stared hard at his reflection and shook his head. Feelings that were supposed to have vanished, or at least dissipated, were bubbling—boiling—under the surface and . . . he couldn't breathe. He tapped the mirror. "All you know is how to get in trouble."

He redressed, frowning, and checked his phone. His stomach sank again and he clicked away the calendar reminder it was Pete's rehearsal dinner. *These* were the feelings he should have been confused about tonight. His childhood friend, his ex sweetheart, was getting married soon.

Right now, they'd be at the restaurant, possibly about to deliver speeches.

Shaky, guilty fingers prodded his phone and Carl's voice cracked when Jason answered. "Ah, Jase. Guess you're about to head to the rehearsal dinner?"

A floorboard creaked outside the bathroom and Carl screwed his eyes tight. "Look, I know this is . . . would you . . . keep me on the phone during the toasts? Secretly? I . . . I just want . . ."

"To torture yourself?"

Except, that wasn't quite it. He swallowed thickly. "To be there. From a distance."

A soft knock came at the bathroom door, and Grayson murmured from the other side, "What's going on, Carl. Talk to me."

Carl pressed the phone so hard against his ear, he could feel the beat of his racing pulse through it.

He shuffled to the door, caught and released his breath, and opened, flashing an upbeat smile.

Grayson stood in the hallway in his big fluffy dressing gown, holding two cups of steaming tea. He eyed Carl's smile suspiciously. "Shall we sit?"

Carl followed him back to the dining table, where they sat opposite one another and sipped. Grayson looked questioningly from Carl to the phone he held.

"I-I'm facing things," Carl stammered. And he *was*, yet . . . something inside him was yelling that he wasn't facing the *right* things.

He shoved the voice away. "It's my ex's rehearsal dinner. I've asked my brother to keep his phone on."

Grayson nodded slowly, shoulders slumping slightly. He stared at his tea. "You can hear everything?"

"There's a lot of background noise, but I can hear when Jason speaks." Carl's stomach twisted.

They sipped silently for some minutes, Carl swapping his phone from ear to ear. He could hear parts of conversations and general chatter, but he was only half focused. The other half of himself was viscerally aware of Grayson and the taut air of unspoken things between them. The goosebumps rumbling over his arms and prickling the back of his neck—

They were all due to him.

He swallowed thickly.

Grayson looked over at the same time, gaze hooking at Carl's throat before climbing up to his eyes. "You haven't got those feelings out of your system, have you?"

Carl swiped a nervous tongue over his bottom lip, crunched his face in concentration, as if Jason had said something worth paying attention to.

Grayson murmured, "What if . . . I don't want you to?"

The words slammed painfully into Carl's chest, sending it into a fluttering ruckus. He swallowed, and swallowed, and his voice was lost, trapped under the heart beating up his throat. "I . . . I . . ."

Almost simultaneously, another ruckus happened down the line. The crisp sound of piano keys. Whirling music. It blasted through the phone, close. So close, it could only be Jason playing. And if Jason was playing in front of everyone at the rehearsal dinner—

Carl stood abruptly.

The room was spinning. With every rippled note, the truth was emerging.

"Oh shit. Oh God." His fingers were a mess over the phone screen as he prodded and prodded to end the call, only to ring again. The phone was buzzing and buzzing, and Jason was not picking up.

"Come on, come on."

Grayson rose and rounded the table. "What happened? What's going on?"

Carl shook his phone, as if that could make his brother pick up. He looked desperately at Grayson, shaking. "I—I have to go home. Right now. They've figured out Jason isn't me. That means . . . that means everyone'll know. My ex. My mum—"

Grayson took Carl's shaking limbs into a cradling embrace.

"I can't run anymore, Grayson. I have to . . ."

Grayson rubbed his back warmly. "Deep breaths. I'll book tickets. I'll drive you to the airport."

Carl continued to tremble, and Grayson steered him through each step; returning to Jason's villa, finding his passport, purchasing the last seat on the next flight to Melbourne, packing his things, driving him to the airport.

"I'm afraid," Carl murmured into their farewell embrace.

A soft kiss landed atop his head. "I believe in you."

"Take good care of these friends of mine, and I will go at once to fight the monster."

L. Frank Baum

The Wonderful Wizard of Oz

Chapter Sixteen

The light kiss on his head felt like a shield. It infiltrated his veins, tingling through him. Like he'd drunk a courageous potion.

It gave Carl strength.

He flew to Melbourne, then to Tassie, then bussed all the way to Earnest Point, arriving to the scene he'd once painted for Grayson: sunshine over quaint cottages and colourful gardens with falling autumn leaves.

It looked even prettier than he'd remembered it, and except for the storm of anxiety brewing in his stomach—and in his heart—no one could wish a pleasanter home.

A gust whooshing over the town square sprayed fountain water over Carl's face. He chuckled. Not the first time that'd happened! What a proper welcome.

He wiped it off with his sleeve, and his chuckle froze as he glimpsed Cora in her signature red crossing the street—

She halted on the footpath, scarf fluttering around her, a bright magazine crushed against her chest. Eyes that Carl had looked into a million times held his, and filled with tears.

Ten seconds, twenty. Neither could move.

I believe in you.

Carl swallowed thickly, and took a wobbly first step towards her.

THEY TALKED FOR A LONG TIME—UNTIL THE AIR HAD CHILLED, and their embraces became buffers against the wind. A conversation he'd dreaded and avoided and run away from. One single conversation, and they were fundamentally changed. In the space of a few honest words, they'd become closer. Formed the beginnings of a new bond.

"Mum," he said a couple of times, and Cora began weeping.

"Patricia's your real mum. She raised you."

"Yeah. But indulge me this once? I've wanted to say it for years."

"I've secretly wanted to hear it, too." She hugged him fiercely, the magazine she held slipping to Carl's lap as she peppered sweet little kisses atop his head. He squeezed her back. Tight, tighter. He wouldn't let her go.

She laughed again and pulled back, swiping the dribbling mascara off her face. "I always thought horoscopes were silly, fun nonsense I indulged in. I never thought they could be so right." She prodded a finger at the magazine on Carl's lap. "It said something great would happen. Something I'd cherish for the rest of my life." She laughed even as more tears streamed down her face. "Both my sons have acknowledged me. Forgiven me."

Sons.

He closed his eyes on the heaving warmth in his chest. It was almost too much, and he curled one hand tight, feeling the ghost of Grayson's in his like he had while practicing this conversation. "You and me, we have lots in common."

He picked up the magazine, flicked through it, and read out the fateful horoscope while sneaking peeks at her joyous, laughing face.

"See? Pretty insightful. What's yours?"

Carl glanced over his own, nodded, and snapped the magazine shut.

"What does it say?" Cora asked, nabbing the magazine back. "Is it apt?"

Like it could've been written about him. "It's got a lot of integrity, this one. I know what I have to do."

"Ah, talk to Pete," Cora said. "Have you seen him yet?"

Carl shook his head.

"Well. Speak of the devil." She was looking over his shoulder, and Carl held his breath and turned around.

Pete and Nick were walking around the fountain, hand-in-hand. When Pete spotted him, he murmured something to his fiancé and moved alone towards Carl.

Cora gave him another quick peck as she rose. "I'd best leave you to it."

Pete wore casual jeans and a grim smile; Carl had seen this smile once or twice in their many years knowing one another, and it meant Carl was in the proverbial doghouse.

He tensed on the park bench and Pete plunked himself at the other end, leaving a good amount of space between them. Something that might, a year ago, have felt like a punch to his gut, but today . . . today it didn't bother Carl at all. He could've done with *more* distance.

Pete scrolled an assessing eye over him. "You look wrecked."

"I came straight from the airport."

There was an acknowledging glance at Carl's suitcase, and a tight nod.

"I thought you were acting off these last few weeks. I couldn't understand your sudden fascination with the sergeant. Turns out, it wasn't you at all."

Carl wished, *desperately* wished, he'd practiced this conversation with Grayson, too. He swallowed and ran a hand through his hair.

"Why?" Pete asked.

Carl blurted, "I was pretending I was okay with it. That it didn't hurt every time I saw you together. But, back then, it did hurt. And I couldn't bear being your best man, so I . . ."

"Dreamed up the insane plot to have your brother act in your stead?"

"It seemed like a good idea at the time."

"Why didn't you tell me it was too much?"

Carl paused at this, frowned, and slowly met Pete's gaze. "Why didn't you know?"

The disappointment in Pete's eyes shifted to uncertainty and he looked away, swallowing. "You're right. I should have." His brow crunched. "I was so lost in Nick, I . . . I became selfish."

"You became selfish, and I became stupid. I'm sorry for lying to you, Pete."

After a few quiet moments, Pete murmured, "Did I break your heart badly?"

Carl's throat stung. "At first it seemed dashed to pieces. Irreparable."

"At first?"

"I've had a lot of conversations over the last few weeks. Each one has been piecing it back together. Not only fixing it but making it stronger. Now it beats harder than it ever has before."

Pete observed him quietly.

Carl had been reflecting on those conversations; he hadn't realised he was smiling. He fingered the curve at his lips, and it deepened.

"Who's that for?" Pete asked.

Carl looked over at him, and laughed. He stood and took hold of his suitcase.

Carl spent the night in his own house and had dreams, lots of them, all of Grayson in grey, staring at him with insanely dark eyes. Carl kept running towards him, but every time he got close, *poof,* the guy vanished. It was all extremely irritating. So close to toppling into him, so close to a few moments of pleasantness . . . Honestly, it was like Dream Grayson was teasing him. There was even the quirk of his lips each time Carl narrowly missed flattening him to the ground.

Carl woke cursing the Scorpio for stirring him up. Grayson would have to take responsibility for this.

So he texted Grayson something along those lines.

It wasn't enough. There was something else he had to do.

He found his trusty bike, pumped up the flat tires, and raced into town. As he hit the centre, his convenience store in sight, a familiar, spine-chilling "Oi!" had him coming to a whooshing, tire-squealing halt.

Oh, hell. Not even twenty-four hours, and he'd already incurred the wrath of Sergeant Owen.

"What have I done now?"

Owen folded his arms. "You're back, I see."

"And despite falling for my twin, you're set to give me another ticket?" Carl looked around, trying to figure out what he'd done wrong.

Knuckles rapped his helmet. "I stopped you out of sheer shock. You're wearing one of these."

Carl hopped off his bike, leaned it against a bike stand and took Toto off. He'd been surprised to see Grayson's trusty red helmet stowed away inside his luggage. And unnerved. Had Grayson thought of this as a parting gift? In case Carl . . .

He crushed the helmet close to his chest, like it was one of those popping-out hearts that he was trying to rein back in. This was why he was racing here. He needed to see Jason. Tell him he'd got himself in a few predicaments back in Wellington. Get his okay about things. Tell him he was going back.

Ideally, he should've barged into his neighbour's place last night and talked then, he'd be halfway back by now. But . . . Sergeant Owen could be scary. He'd glimpsed the two entering their place entangled in one another's arms, and wisely decided against interrupting.

Said neighbour, the town policeman, his soon-to-be-in-law-probably, was still speaking. ". . . you."

"What?"

A slow blink. "You haven't changed *that* much. I was saying thank you."

"You're thanking me?"

"For being an idiot and thereby making me the happiest man in the world. Your brother—" Owen's smile dazzled. "He's quite something."

"Quite something?"

"My everything."

Carl was all out of sorts. He wasn't used to Sergeant Owen without a chastising frown. But if it meant fewer tickets in future, and if it meant Jason had found love and was happy . . .

He smiled and nodded.

Owen shook his head. "Off you go."

Carl dashed for his convenience store.

"I also am well-pleased with my new heart; and really, that was the only thing I wished in all the world."

L. Frank Baum

The Wonderful Wizard of Oz

Chapter Seventeen

He was coming clean.

It'd been half a day and a night travelling back to Wellington, and it was very early in the morning, but Carl had decided this.

First, though, he had to see Grayson. He couldn't wait any longer.

He dried his shower-damp hair and opened Jason's wardrobe. His gaze skated past all the suits and clinging tops and settled on the suitcase he'd stuffed in there.

A pair of comfy jeans and his comfier flannel hoodie later, he headed into a crisp morning and followed blazing lampposts to Over The Raindough. He caught a glimpse of his reflection in the glass window, and he squared his shoulders and nodded at himself. The red and black checkered flannel, the worn-in jeans, the sneakers. Perfect. He totally exuded *himself*.

He knocked on the door and his chest pounded as a form moved behind the fogged glass. The door opened, sucking in air over him, and revealed . . .

Sage. In an apron and hair net, flour dusted along her cheek. She smiled brightly. "You're here early. Come in."

Carl went in, breathing in the scent of baking bread, and scanned the kitchen. "Is Grayson not working?"

Sage "ahhhed" as she rounded the counter and began making coffee. "You're here to see him." Her smile twitched. "Poppy really had no chance."

She sure was sharp.

"He won't be in today," she continued. "Not sure when he'll be back, to be honest."

Carl snapped his gaze to hers.

She slid a coffee over to him. "He said he had somewhere he needed to be, and left last night after saying goodbye."

Carl's breath caught and electricity jolted through him over and over. Grayson had somewhere he needed to be. . . . *You haven't got those feelings out of your system, have you? What if I don't want you to?*

Carl yanked out his phone and tried to call. Couldn't get through. Maybe his phone was on airplane mode. Or drained of battery after the legs to Tasmania and up to Earnest Point.

Had they passed one another in an airport without knowing?

"Are you all right?" Sage asked, eying Carl restlessly pacing the length of the counter.

Carl laughed, heavy and deep. "Grayson makes me ridiculously happy."

"You joined the admiration club?"

More laughter. "Became king of it."

"You're not worried he'll turn you down? Break your heart?"

"He was the one who fixed it for me. If he wants to break it, only he is allowed."

"Why are you so happy he left?"

Carl stopped pacing and focused on Sage, who was watching him curiously, trying to put it all together. But she was missing a few key pieces of information. Information Carl well and truly owed her. He perched on a stool and nervously cupped his coffee. "I'm happy because I know where he went."

"Where?"

"A small town in Tasmania."

"He's in Oz?"

Another wave of elation shook Carl, and he nodded.

"Why's he there?"

Carl let out a stomach-tightening breath and looked Sage in the eye. "He's there because that's where I live."

"You live . . . I thought you lived round the corner?" Sage's frown had Carl gulping a massive load of guilt.

"My twin, Jason, lives around the corner."

"Jason—" Sage dropped her coffee and it spilled in a puddle between them. "You're not Jason Lyall?"

Carl bowed his head. "I'm his twin. His evil twin. I took his identity and fooled you all."

Sage was quiet. Carl's stomach churned.

"I'm sorry."

Sage laughed, trying to sound upbeat, but Carl felt the hollowness, the hurt. "I was too silly to figure it out, huh?"

He shook his head. "I don't like you thinking of yourself as silly, Sage. I hated anyone who suggested that. It punched me in the gut every time. It was why I pretended to be Jason in the first place. To stick it to those damn mums."

Sage stared.

Carl pushed on. "They criticise you, make fun of you, and I understood what that felt like, because I've experienced the same, and I . . . I wanted to prove them wrong. I wanted you to know famous Jason. I wanted to pretend I could *be* someone like him."

Carl slammed his eyes shut. "You and I may not be university educated, or know all the big historical events, we may struggle to solve riddles, but we're colourful and curious. We're kind. That's what the people who love us value most."

He opened his eyes to Sage blinking rapidly. She swiped at her eye. "Gah, I should be upset at *you* right now. But I'm only upset. This is it, exactly. I often feel so much less than others; the typical blonde. Head full of straw. Those careless words have a way of drowning my spirits, but I shouldn't care. I won't. Kindness is most important, and that's . . . that's why I forgive you, Evil Twin of Jason Lyall. You lied, but it stemmed from pain and the kindness to want to help."

Carl swallowed thickly. "My name's Carl Birch. I run a convenience store in a small town in Tasmania."

Sage reached over. "Nice to meet you, Carl."

He shook her hand, and she pulled him closer over the counter, a sparkle of curiosity in her eye. "Why is Grayson at your home? Since when does it make you grin stupidly? Gimme all the details."

Carl threw his head back and laughed. She was his kind of gossipy friend. He leaned in, and told her everything.

"You're in Wellington," Grayson rumbled down the line.

After a day trying, Carl finally got through. He reclined in a chair on the veranda and stared out at moon-dappled heads of lavender. "I left something here."

"Something important?"

"Something I'd rather not live without."

A hitched breath. "Ah, my good looks."

Carl flicked at a head of lavender, grinning. "And *most* of your personality."

Laughter tinkered down the phone line.

"You went to Earnest Point," Carl murmured.

"Your text said you wanted to catch me and never let go."

Carl flushed and sank deeper into his seat, staring up at the night sky that Grayson was possibly looking up at too. "I had a rather vexing dream."

"Good. It made me buy a ticket right away. I wanted you to know, to see, to feel that . . . you've already caught me."

Carl swallowed, whispered, "Both of us dashing off after one another . . . It says everything, doesn't it?"

"We probably should have a conversation about it."

"Yes. And—"

"And?"

"Let's have it face to face."

On the day of the talent show, Carl was a bundle of nerves. He was helping Sage in the kitchen, plating green-frosted cupcakes. He'd promised Sage that when she went into the main hall, he'd encourage Leo on stage for his piano performance, and he was hyper-aware that Grayson had landed and was Ubering home this very moment.

Finally. The days apart had felt endless. Carl had bubbled with anticipation, and went on a hell of a lot of bike rides with Toto. This morning he'd gone to Houghton Bay and day-dreamed about Grayson emerging from the surf in sparkles . . . Then he'd closed his eyes and imagined Grayson in his house in Earnest Point, while he waited for his connection. Hopefully Grayson had made himself at home. Cooked meals in his kitchen, slept in his bed, snooped in all his drawers . . .

"Carl? Hello? Anyone home?"

Carl sighed. "Soon, very soon."

Sage snorted. People were finding their seats; the show was set to start in five minutes. "Leo's due on stage in fifteen." After the witches' sons showed off their talents. Carl gave her two thumbs up, and as soon as she left, panicked. He checked the foyer, and the outside quad, and the gardens near the gate. "Leo, where are you?"

A snicker had him whisking around to smirky faces. The two witches' sons were hopping off a shiny electric bike. "Probably wet his pants and went off to cry in a dirty corner," one said.

White-haired Linda, in a golden shawl, shuffled through the gate past them, flanked by a few friends. She eyed the boys and caught Carl's gaze with an acknowledging nod. "Today you'll get what you deserve."

The other bully scoffed, and Carl murmured for Linda to enjoy the talent show. She entered the hall, and one of the witches came outside with a grim smile. "Talents. Line up behind the stage curtain."

Ah!

Leo, where are you? God, what wouldn't he give for Grayson to show up now. He'd know exactly where to look! Wouldn't be floundering around like Carl.

"Carl?"

"Not now, I'm busy." He peered around a large tree.

"Busy doing what?"

"Looking for—" Carl startled and whipped around to Leo watching him curiously, his head cocked. "There you are!" He tripped over a tree root, caught himself, and hauled Leo into a hug. "You had me worried. Thought you were getting stage fright."

"I was getting stage fright."

"Then I'm back to worrying."

"I threw up in the bathroom. There might be more to come."

"Why didn't you tell me? I could have—"

"Helped me throw up?"

A wince. "Prepared a hot towel?" Carl patted both Leo's

shoulders. "I'm sorry you're feeling nervous. If you really don't want to—"

"I do. I *will*." The insistence. The determination.

Carl admired Leo and rubbed his hair. "Channeling some Jason Lyall courage there?"

"No. Some Carl courage."

Warmth unfurled in his stomach. "I'm hardly courageous."

"You've stood up for me and Mum since the beginning. If I can be a little like you, I'd be very happy. You're my hero."

Carl's throat got tight and his chest fluttered. He went in for another hug—

"No more!" Leo squeaked. "I really might throw up."

They laughed, and Carl led him inside—

Into another drama that was playing out in the foyer—right next to the counter separating the kitchen, where a few plates of the freshly iced cupcakes waited.

Carl halted Leo inside the doorway and took in the scene. Three witches, all talking at once to a policeman while the two bullies shrank into the corner. The mums of the boys were furious—at their sons, and the man in uniform—and were begging to be allowed to stay until the event was over before they headed to the station.

"You have to understand. This won't run without us."

"That's a bone you'll have to pick with your children. Come on."

One of the mums whirled to the third. "You'll have to take over as MC."

The cowering boys threw themselves at their mums. "Please! Please, we didn't mean it. We'd have returned the bike later."

The policeman spoke into his walkie-talkie for his partner to come in, then to the boys. "Up you get."

"Noooo!" The boys yelled and pushed frantically, and in

the process, the witches stumbled. It was like dominoes. One fell into the other, who fell into the other, who fell into—

Carl sucked in a sharp breath.

The cupcakes!

Two plates went flying off the counter; green icing rained down on the third witch's face, her pristine white shirt.

She shrieked and smeared gobs of icing, trying to get it off her. "Look what you've done! How can I go on stage now?"

"Quickly, go home and shower—"

"The show is *starting*. The only person left is . . ."

The witches all stared at one another in horror.

The doors to the main hall swung open and Sage strode out as if summoned. She froze at the incredible sprawling scene at her feet. She blinked a few times, and Carl absolutely caught the quirk of her cheek before she quickly swallowed a smirk. "Are you all right?" she asked, offering a hand to help up the green-frosted witch.

"You'll have to take over running the show," one of the mums said tightly. "Our kids' act won't take place either. You'll have to find someone to fill in."

A head swung Carl's way. "You. The piano—"

Carl widened his eyes, and Sage stepped in front of him. "I'll make sure the event runs smoothy. I can take over from here."

She gestured to the policeman, who inclined his head and frog-marched the mothers and sons out. The last witch stomped on a cupcake and huffed out of the hall after them.

Leo poked his tongue at her back as she left, and Carl nodded. "Let's not ever tell them the truth."

"Good. I'll play in their slot. That'll give you a few more minutes to find another performance."

Sage cleared away the smooshed cupcakes, and Carl hurried to help her.

“We lost eight,” he counted. “But thanks to your foresight to make a dozen extra, we still have plenty.”

“I have to get inside.”

“Go ahead. Don’t fret about the extra performance. I have an idea.”

Sage smiled and skipped off to run the show, Leo readied himself to play his piano piece, and Carl made a call.

Carl stood at the side of the main hall, clapping hard towards the neon-lit stage where Leo finished a jolly piano piece and bowed. “En core!” Carl hollered and clapped some more.

Leo came off the stage in an exhilarated rush and zoomed to Carl, breathless. “I did all right!”

“You did awesome! A right Chopin, you are.”

“Do you know Chopin?”

“Didn’t he do Chop—sticks?”

Leo sighed and patted his back. “How you ever fooled anyone . . .”

Sage crossed the stage, enamoured the audience with a few funny lines, and gazed to the side, where the bullies’ replacement act waited in the wings.

Carl bit down on a massive grin and threw an arm around Leo’s shoulders. “This next act should scare the bejeesus out of us.”

Sage left the microphone, music filtered through the speaker, and Grayson made himself visible to Carl for a second time that day. The first time had been a fleeting rush, ushering him into place, barely space to breathe him in; but now . . .

Now, Carl got a very good view, and he sucked in a lot of air.

In gleaming silver shoes, Jason’s jacket that Carl had lost to him in a gust, and a familiar scarf covered in wee mice that shimmered under the stage lights, Grayson tapped his way across the stage.

Carl's heart leaped with the infectious rhythm and Grayson's mesmerising confidence. Precision and grace, clappity-clap. Twisting, turning, tappity tap. Grayson danced like he was happy. Like his heart was full.

Like he could feel Carl's was the same.

From the stage, Grayson's gaze landed on him, a gleam of those dark eyes . . .

Carl could never get enough. He watched in shivers.

WHEN THEY WERE DONE, WHEN THE TALENTS ALL HEADED UP TO the stage for a second bow, Carl slunk out of the hall. On his way to deliver the cupcakes, he paused at the pictures of alumni on the walls. His finger traced over the faces to the one that shared Grayson's smile.

Carl stepped close and whispered, like Grayson's mother could hear him. "I like him a lot, Mrs Woods. Rather desperately, actually. But one mustn't say that too loud. His ego might—"

Warm laughter hit his nape, warmer hands pulled him around, and the warmest smile landed on him.

"You snuck after me rather fast."

"After you? I'm starved from the flight, I'm after the cupcakes."

Hand balled in that soft silver scarf, Carl hauled Grayson closer.

Noses grazed; breaths caught.

Carl was meant to show some restraint—have this conversation later, after the event, certainly not in the moments before cupcakes needed to be trucked to tables. But Grayson was here, standing right before him with shiny shoes and shinier eyes, and he couldn't hold back.

He pressed his lips against Grayson's, and through the tingles, murmured, "I haven't got those feelings out of my system. And I don't want to."

Dark eyes bored through his and arms locked around his waist as if to make absolutely sure he wouldn't run away again.

Carl tugged at Grayson's scarf. "I've been thinking about it—the moments that built up this feeling. This scarf . . ." He smiled at the little mice all over it. "You were feeling sick that night, but you gave me this to keep me warm."

"You liked the chivalry."

"I liked the pattern."

A raised brow.

"A man who even likes field mice . . ." Carl beheld the deepening affection in those dark eyes. "That had to be a good, kind man."

A swallow bulged in Grayson's throat, like his voice had become stuck by a heart beating there. Carl understood and traced the line down his neck, smiling—

Grayson kissed him.

"I'm so glad to be at home again."

L. Frank Baum

The Wonderful Wizard of Oz

Epilogue

Carl would never think of himself as a Dead-End Dude again. Even if someone came up and said it to his face, criticised his selection of magazines for their lack of journalistic integrity, he'd simply let it go. Forget it.

He *ran* his own convenience store. It had all the daily—and emergency—necessities for his beloved Earnest Pointers, and townies loved to come in and share all the local goss with him. Not only did he have a stable job as his own boss, and have friends, and an—even bigger—family, he had Grayson.

Who had left Wellington to be with Carl. Who'd quickly won the hearts of the locals. Who, between an eclectic array of jobs, always popped into his store for some PDA.

How much more exciting could his life get?

Carl smirked and flipped the page of the mag he was perusing for the next set of horoscopes. He and Cora had been giggling over them during a coffee break, and Carl was still going strong. "Oh, this is relevant. I really do have a courageous Leo coming to visit soon. He and his mum are arriving next week."

"You talk about this Leo like you've half adopted him."

"I suppose I have. I'd like it if he thought of me as his fun uncle."

"His troublesome one, you mean."

Carl pretended he didn't hear that, and smirked.

"Read out Grayson's," Cora said, rubbing her hands eagerly. "Let's see what it says about your man."

Carl held up the magazine and cleared his throat. "Scorpio. Totally smitten with his Capricorn boyfriend and committed to love him for a lifetime."

Cora laughed, shaking her head. "It does not say that."

"It might as well." The voice came from the door, and Carl snapped himself around, gazing at Grayson as he came in. He blinked, and shook his head. Unreal. Absolutely unreal. How was it sunshine actually glittered behind this guy of his?

Good thing Grayson had moved here, leaving his groupies behind, or there'd be swooning left and right. Carl had enough of a job making sure everyone in town knew this man was his. His lips were chaffed dry.

Cora snagged the mag from him. "I'll see myself out." She hurried past, giving Grayson the biggest smile on her way, and Grayson returned it, murmuring she should pop around for dinner later.

Carl's heart went berserk, beating all the way up his throat. How easily Grayson fit in here. How comfortable they were.

Grayson's dark gaze hit him; Carl leapt over the counter in a flap of flannel and catapulted into opening arms—

Oof. The tackling hug was more enthusiastic than either anticipated; Grayson toppled with the force of it and they crumpled into a laughing heap on the store floor.

Carl stared down at his man admiringly, while Grayson's laugh vibrated warmly through him.

"Since the first time we met," Grayson murmured, "we haven't stopped falling."

"All part of our journey."

Grayson lifted up and kissed Carl softly. "And look where we ended up."

"Happy."

"*Home*."

THE END

About the author

A bit about me: I'm a big, BIG fan of slow-burn romances. I love to read and write stories with characters who slowly fall in love.

Some of my favorite tropes to read and write are: Enemies to Lovers, Friends to Lovers, Clueless Guys, Bisexual, Pansexual, Demisexual, Oblivious MCs, Everyone (Else) Can See It, Slow Burn, Love Has No Boundaries.

I write a variety of stories, Contemporary MM Romances with a good dollop of angst, Contemporary lighthearted MM Romances, and even a splash of fantasy.
My books have been translated into German, Italian, French, Spanish, and Thai.

Contact: http://www.anytasunday.com/about-anyta/
Sign up for Anyta's newsletter and receive a free e-book:
http://www.anytasunday.com/newsletter-free-e-book/

Join my Facebook group to chat all things Slow Burn Romance:
https://www.facebook.com/groups/SlowBurnSundays/

You can also find me here:
www.anytasunday.com
anytasunday@gmail.com

For information about new releases and freebies, follow me on BookBub:
https://www.bookbub.com/authors/anyta-sunday

www.ingramcontent.com/pod-product-compliance
Lightning Source LLC
LaVergne TN
LVHW091408190726
843491LV00006B/1329

* 9 7 8 3 9 4 7 9 0 9 7 1 1 *